MW01166990

Bright Christmas

An Amish Love Story

SUSAN ROHRER

Infinite Arts Media

BRIGHT CHRISTMAS: An Amish Love Story
(Redeeming Romance Series)
Written by Susan Rohrer, adapted from her screenplay

Kindly direct inquiries about novel or screenplay to:
InfiniteArtsMgmt@gmail.com

Readers may contact author at:
shelfari.com/susanrohrer

Public domain lyrics appear from the following:
"Joyful, Joyful, We Adore Thee" by Henry J. van Dyke; *"Joy to the World"* by Isaac Watts; *"O Little Town of Bethlehem"* by Phillips Brooks; *"I Heard the Bells on Christmas Day"* by Henry W. Longfellow

Cover Images: Sandra Martin Hudgins
Cover Graphic Design: Lynda Jakovich, cooldogdesign

ISBN 13: 978-1484972656
ISBN 10: 1484972651

Published in the United States of America

First Edition 2013

To all who endeavor to live
in true faith, hope, and love

contents

one

Charity Bright gathered firewood from a dwindling stack, her gaze drawn to the horizon. Try as she might, she simply couldn't shake the sensation that enveloped her. Something was in the air. It wasn't just the scent of fresh cut hickory and ash. No, it was far more. A whisper penetrated her being.

Change was coming.

How could something be so fearsome and yet so fascinating? Perhaps it was because, within their Old Order Amish district, change wasn't an everyday—even an every year—thing. Change took time. It meandered like the brook bordering their property, imperceptibly carving its path. For the most part, Charity preferred it that way. It was comforting to know what to expect. Tomorrow would dawn soon enough.

She didn't make a fuss over birthdays, least of all her own. But this particular one—it seemed different somehow. When the sun set, then rose again, it would mean much more than simply bidding a fond farewell to her teens. There was an invisible corner she'd turn. In the morning, she'd be twenty. She'd awaken to find that the adventure of her adult life had finally begun.

Charity nestled the load of split logs into the sturdy black fabric of her everyday apron. This had been the warmest autumn in memory, so she drank in the new crispness of the air, and the Yuletide it heralded. Many favored the warmth or color of other seasons, but for Charity, there was something about the frosty Pennsylvania winters that made them the most beautiful of all. How she relished the wind's chill, the refreshing tingle against her face and hands.

She gazed at her surroundings. They had a good life. Smoke curled from the chimney of her family's wood-framed home. A light breeze dissipated the rising puffs into a brilliant blue sky. A milking cow grazed beside their red barn, the bell about her neck softly clanking with each step. In a way, she longed to preserve it all, just as it stood, forever.

But that was not to be.

Charity flapped the hem of her apron over her load of oak and maple, then headed back toward the house. She ducked as a stone sailed over her head. It landed across the yard inside a bushel basket, set atop a fence post. Nearing seventeen, her twin brothers, Aaron and Isaac, still found time to play.

"Yes!" Aaron pumped his fists.

Charity suppressed her amusement. "You two are far braver than I am, piffling around—so idle—what with Christmas coming and Dat on his way home to catch you."

Almost in tandem, the boys whirled to check the road for their father's return. "No sign yet," Isaac said.

Aaron sidled up to her. "You wouldn't tattle on your own brothers, would you, Charity?"

Wryly, she tipped her head. "No need. The size of the woodpile will do the telling." Though she was the eldest, she reminded herself to exercise that role lightly with her brothers. She was not their mother and didn't presume to be.

Out of the corner of her eye, she watched as, with no protest other than trading a chagrined grimace, Aaron and Isaac picked up their axes. Compliantly, they trudged back to their task at the chopping block. As competitive as the two of them were, no doubt, they would resume their stone-tossing contest just as soon as their chores were done.

Indeed, by now, their father would be traversing the rolling hills from town with their grandfather, in the family's horse-drawn buggy. How deeply she respected her father. Everyone did. The name, Nathan Bright, was associated with handcrafted furniture every bit as sturdy as his character. No wonder Mamm had married Dat.

Charity counted back. This was the seventeenth December since Mamm had slipped into eternity. Yet, even after the grave, Dat had chosen to remain true to her.

As she stoked the fire inside, Charity brushed back the slender ribbons of her white kapp, lest they be scorched by the blaze. How dearly she prized that covering, the last of the kapps Mamm had pleated with her own hands. Dat had surprised her with it when she'd turned eighteen—two years ago, now. At the time, Dat didn't explain what the gift meant in so many words. Still, she understood. He was telling her that, even though she was unmarried, she could set aside the black kapp of her youth. Every day she pinned that white kapp in place, she was taking on the mantle of her mother.

There was something about the aroma of apple butter bubbling on the stove that always invigorated Charity. Perhaps it was the imported cinnamon she ground, or maybe the nutmeg, both contributed by their neighbors to the south, the Beachey family. While her closest friend, Bethany Beachey, worked at her side, Charity wordlessly acknowledged a secret to herself.

It might just be the apples.

They'd been harvested that fall, then dutifully delivered, straight to her kitchen door, by the Yoder's strappingly handsome son, Daniel.

Ah, yes. Daniel Yoder.

There were many Yoders in their community, but keeping her wits whenever this particular Yoder was around, well, that took discipline. She did her best not to let her gaze linger on him, what with his wheat colored hair and those chestnut eyes. That ready smile of his—with those crescent dimples on either side—those alone could tip her completely off balance.

Bethany scooped out an apple core. "Why are you smiling like that?"

Charity bit at her lower lip. "Am I?"

"You're thinking of him, aren't you?"

Feeling a blush rise, Charity averted her gaze. She scraped the nutmeg into a measuring cup.

"You're practically twenty, Charity. It's not like it's a sin."

"I know." Wait. Had she put in the ginger yet? Yes. There were the dashes of tan in the mixture.

Bethany shook her head. "Half of our friends are already published and married. You won't even come to the singings."

"I will."

Bethany leaned closer. "When?"

Charity dumped the spice mixture into the kettle. "Oh, I don't know. Sometime. There's so much to do around here." That was true, especially now with Christmas on the way and their canned goods flying off the shelves in town.

Bethany shrugged with that crooked little grin of hers. She was pretty good at knowing when to drop a hot potato.

Anyway, it wasn't like Charity hadn't noticed Daniel's appeal long ago, as they'd both come of age. She'd just always reminded herself not to indulge herself too soon with thoughts of him.

Not yet.

Admittedly, it had been a bit harder to resist thoughts of Daniel this past harvest than in previous years. She'd chased envy away as several of her younger friends' pairings had been published to the church. The announcements seemed endless last fall, then—just to add to the awkwardness of it—Rhoda Chupp wondered aloud why Charity's name still wasn't on the list. Rhoda was getting on in years and very hard of hearing. Her pronounced whispers could be heard clear across a cornfield.

Of course, Rhoda hadn't meant any harm, but something had still twisted in Charity's stomach. There'd been no escaping all those eyes that darted into her direction. Where was a trap door to crawl through when she needed it?

Oh, to simply disappear.

Just concentrate on being happy for the others, she'd told herself, but it had been no use. Rhoda's comment kept rattling around. To this day, it still rang in her ears.

True, she'd rarely taken the time to go to the singings, even when she'd known Daniel would be there, with so many girls surely vying for his attention. When Aaron and Isaac asked her to ride with them last weekend, her heart had begged her to indulge itself. Somehow she'd heard herself decline, almost like someone else's voice had come out of her body. *Just a little longer,* she'd thought. *Just wait.* When she turned twenty—with her brothers grown and the weight of responsibility on Dat lighter— there'd be time enough to pursue such things.

Tomorrow, that day would come.

Contentedly, Charity peeled the crisp fruit. The fresh aroma filled her nostrils. She offered a bit of the peeling to Bethany. Her favorite part.

Bethany popped the treat into her mouth, then grinned back, the green apple peel covering her teeth.

Charity chuckled. Whenever there was the least bit of a bump between them, Bethany sure knew how to get over it. What a pleasure it was to have a friend like her around. She always found ways to make even the most mundane work fun.

Bethany was a blessing Charity often counted in her life. Like almost all of her immediate family, Bethany's face was lightly dashed with freckles, set off by a torrent of copper curls that refused to stay in place, particularly when it rained or if she were anywhere near a steaming kettle.

It stymied her that Bethany's name had never been on the list of published couples either, as much as Bethany hoped to find love. Why couldn't anyone see what a good wife she'd be?

Charity grabbed another apple. "How did things go for you at the singing Sunday night?"

"He was there, again," Bethany beamed.

"And...?"

"We had a nice conversation. I almost thought he'd ask to take me home, but... Maybe next time."

Bethany hadn't mentioned a name, but Charity knew exactly who had Bethany's hopes fluttering:

Levi Hooley.

Bethany longed for Levi to notice her. That was no secret. Not with the way Bethany enthused over each and every time Levi tipped his hat in passing, or about the growing companionship between their likeminded fathers. Things did look promising.

"I had a dream about him last night." A twinkle danced in Bethany's eyes.

Nobody lit her up like Levi Hooley. "So..."

"So, I dreamed that Levi got all cleaned up, walked clear over to our house, sat my Dat down on the porch, and asked for permission to call on me." Bethany bounced lightly on her toes. Up and down went an escaped curl. "Our secret, okay?"

"I promise." Charity had to admit it. The prospect was exciting. Still, she concealed a measure of concern. The last thing Bethany needed was to have her hopes dashed yet again. Bethany had been to countless singings with as many disappointments. Not once had anyone so much as offered to escort her home in his buggy. Maybe Levi Hooley would be different. Maybe he would be the one for Bethany.

Frankly, Charity couldn't help wondering if Bethany's romantic disappointments didn't owe to Bethany herself so much as they did to her family's progressive persuasions. Bethany's father, Samuel Beachey, was a good Amish man, but he and his brother, Caleb, were part of a scant minority within their community whose convictions were a mite more progressive than most. They'd migrated from a Florida settlement years ago, after a hurricane had leveled their property.

To be sure, the winds of change had blown in with the Beacheys, but their ideas hadn't extended beyond the Beachey's kin.

Not until last year.

All in all, it had been quite a year in their district. Her grandfather was one of their ministers, so Charity had been quietly privy to quite a number of Opa's conversations with Dat. Most had to do with challenges the Beacheys brought to their more conservative way of life. It had been fascinating to listen in, especially after Bethany's Uncle Caleb became the second of their two ministers, alongside Opa, under their bishop.

Bethany's Uncle Caleb hadn't wasted any time putting forth his ideas. First, the Beacheys got the 110-volt electricity they wanted and machines for their dairy business. Next, they got cell phones and a few other approvals. Life settled down after that.

Looking back, Charity marveled. Their world hadn't come to an end. It felt a little like it would, but it hadn't. Bethany was still there with her at the wood stove, helping her put up canned goods the old way, same as always. Dat still made his furniture by hand. Besides the Beacheys, most everyone else continued with their Old Order traditions, just like the Bright and Yoder families.

Apple-scented steam billowed as Bethany stirred the simmering kettle. She tapped a wooden spoon on the rim. "The strange thing is, when I was talking to Levi at the singing—we were chatting right along, having a nice time. At least I thought we were. Then his brother, Reuben, comes up and gives him this bug-eyed kind of look, like..." Bethany bulged her eyes to demonstrate. "And Levi says he has to leave." Bethany set the lid back down on the pot. "Do you think it has anything to do with my Uncle Caleb and all the changes?"

Charity wiped her hands. It was always a bit tough to answer that sort of question with Bethany. "Probably not."

"Probably?"

"You heard the bishop. He told everyone that there shouldn't be any division between any of the families about whatever gets approved."

Bethany hiked a brow. "Oh, I heard. I also heard him say how nobody is supposed to judge anybody about any of it, but I still wonder if they do. Then again, maybe I'm judging them for thinking they're judging me. Then they're judging me back, knowing I'm judging them for judging me." She puffed her cheeks out like a blowfish. "Or...maybe it's just a big screechy cat fight in my head and not really happening at all."

Charity flustered a little. "I guess it's hard to tell when you don't really know for sure what anybody else is thinking. But I don't judge you, Bethany."

"I know."

"Look how conservative we all are, but Dat and Opa, they don't judge your family either. You know you're always welcome here."

There. It was a something of a dodge, but it seemed the only way to answer without getting too far into the one thing they'd agreed to disagree about. Concentrate on chopping. The less said the better.

A knock sounded at the door. Charity's attention snapped toward the entry's window.

Daniel.

Charity transferred a mound of prepared apples into a bowl. "Would you?"

Bethany toweled off her hands, then opened the door. She traded an empty bushel basket for the full one in Daniel's arms. "Thank you, Daniel. I trust you'll refill this one."

Daniel accepted the empty basket in stride. "This and five more in the morning."

Charity cleared a spot on the counter near the sink. It wasn't easy to be so very nonchalant when Daniel Yoder was around. For some reason, it helped to have something to do with her hands. "There's another basket by the fencepost outside, empty except for a few stones, I believe. Tell your mother these will be put up and ready for sale tomorrow."

Daniel smiled back at Charity. "Do you ever stop?"

So. He'd noticed. She returned a wry grin. "I manage to stop on occasion. To sleep."

Daniel nodded pleasantly. "Tomorrow morning, then. After breakfast?"

Charity hoisted the new bushel to the side of the sink for washing. "I'll already be off to town, but the boys will let you in, then."

Disappointment flickered across Daniel's face as he bade them goodbye and closed the door in leaving. Wordlessly, Charity began to pluck out the freshly picked fruit.

Bethany reeled around to Charity, agape. "It's as plain as day that he'd like to call on you. Why do you discourage him?"

Charity bridled a smile as she twisted an apple stem. In a way, it felt good to harness Daniel's appeal. She let it sparkle inside her till the stem broke free. "Bethany, think about it. Have you ever met a man who didn't enjoy pursuit?"

Bethany joined Charity at the window, tracking Daniel as he crossed the yard, past Aaron and Isaac where they added to the woodpile. "You know he's interested and still, you don't—" Just then, the Bright's horse and buggy pulled into view. "Oh, there's your father, now."

Charity watched as Daniel set the bushel basket down and began to help her brothers stack the logs they'd split outside.

Bethany took the sight in. "How long has he been doing this?"

"Doing what?"

Bethany cut her eyes toward the yard. A hint of mischief glimmered. "Pretending that you don't know is not so very far from fibbing."

Charity savored her secret. "Amish men are raised to be helpful."

"There is firewood to be stacked outside plenty of houses around here," Bethany teased. "Why choose yours?"

Charity drifted to the stove, as much to change the subject as to feed the dwindling fire. "Perhaps he has business with my father."

two

Hope Bright pulled her favorite cloche hat down over her shoulder-length tresses, keeping pace with the pedestrian throng. Manhattan traffic was slowed to a near standstill. It was another half a block to the crosswalk and there just wasn't time to go all the way around. Horns blared insistently. Finally, there it was. An opening. She dashed in front of a taxicab and gamely wove her way across the street. Only a true New Yorker would attempt such a thing.

A truck driver rolled down his window to bark at her. "Whaddaya got, a death wish?"

"Sorry!" Hope grinned at the guy as she passed. Men weren't nearly as testy when she was in girlier clothes. But there hadn't been a spare second to change from her sensible shoes or the waitress uniform that hung beneath her warm woolen jacket. Happily, she dashed to the sidewalk stand across the street where a darkly handsome Russian immigrant,

Ivan Kaslov, buffed a businessman's shoes. Ivan would be happy to see her, no matter how she was dressed.

With a squeeze to Ivan's arm, Hope enthused at his customer. "Look at that shine! Have you ever? I can actually see myself in your shoes, like a mirror." Hope hurriedly tugged on Ivan's arm, "Ivan, come on. Let's go!"

Ivan continued to buff the already gleaming shoes. "I have to finish."

Hope fished some cash from her pocket and tucked it into Ivan's. "And that's why this particular shine is on me." Gratefully, the businessman acknowledged his satisfaction. Hope took Ivan's hand and pulled him into a trot. "Come on!"

"Hope, wait!" Ivan called out, but it was to no avail.

Hope only increased her pace. She knew Ivan well enough to guess that he'd match her stride as she ran down the street, dodging pedestrians in her way. "Come on! We're almost there."

Indeed, they were only a few short blocks from her destination. They would not miss what she'd come for, not if she could help it. She skidded to a stop at a rail separating them from the enormous Christmas tree at Rockefeller Center. Just then, a workman on a cherry picker leaned over to place a shimmering star on top.

Energized, Hope turned to Ivan. "See, Ivan? We would have missed it."

Ivan caught his breath. "I think they will leave it up for a while."

Hope shook her head, pointing to the peak of the towering fir. "Not the tree, Silly. The star. It's a very special thing in this city. We'd have missed when they put the star on top."

"Hope, do you think we could—"

"Back home, we didn't put up Christmas trees. Just greenery and candles. Fresh dipped. None of the electric kind."

"That really is great, but I want to—"

"Oh! You know what we should do? We should come skate here, maybe Sunday after—"

All at once, Ivan turned Hope by her shoulders. He drew her into an unexpected kiss. His lips were warm and sweet till he pulled away, holding her face in his hands. "Hope, will you marry me?"

Stunned, Hope struggled to orient herself. She took a step back. "What?"

"Look, I know. It is sudden," Ivan admitted, "but think about it, will you?"

Hope's stomach tightened. Ivan really was a great guy. She'd truly enjoyed his company over the passing months, but there was no way she was ready to get that kind of serious. "Ivan, I... I like you. I really do, but—"

"Many marry on much less," Ivan continued. "Six months, we have known each other."

She stifled a groan. Why couldn't she stop the clock, or better yet turn it back? Sure, she liked him enormously. But marriage? Marriage required a commitment that she just couldn't bring herself to make. "I'm so sorry, Ivan. I just... I can't."

"Hope, I love you. I know we can make this work."

Hope's mind raced. He didn't understand. How could he? Her heart pounded within her. "Look, I don't want to hurt you, Ivan, but..."

This was coming out ridiculously wrong. It sounded so sappy and cliché. Where were the right words? Impossibly lame explanations clamored for her attention. This hadn't been the first time she'd had to curtail a relationship. But Ivan's sweetness made it that much harder than it had been with other guys.

From the beginning, she'd promised herself they'd just stay friends. With most guys that hadn't been a problem, but she could see in Ivan's pooling eyes that, for him, it was. She swallowed, desperate to moisten her parched throat. "I think I need to take a step back from this. From us."

Ivan's lips parted. His head tipped to one side. "From this..." He ran his fingers through his hair. "What is this?"

"I guess it has to be goodbye, Ivan." There, she'd been honest. She'd done the right thing. Now what? How awful was it to leave him when she'd just dragged him away from his work, all the way to Rockefeller Center? Then again, how could she stay? She could not lead him on another moment. Slowly, she willed herself to take a step back. Her other foot quickly followed. "I've got to go." Overwhelmed, she turned and hurried away.

As much as Hope was tempted to look back, she trained her eyes forward. Looking back would not make this parting any easier. That was for certain. Ivan would be standing there, forlorn, begging her to reconsider with those soulful, dark eyes of his. She had learned that much from past experience. A clean break would be best. It was, in fact, the only way.

Hope hurried back across town as fast as her legs would carry her. She turned the final corner. There it was—her safe haven: Manhattan's Café Troubadour. The restaurant had long been her financial constant amidst the ups and downs of musical gigs and off-off Broadway Theater. The place would be teeming with customers. She could throw herself back into her work and regain her emotional footing.

A bell rang as Hope pushed through the Café's front door. Full-figured waitress Myrna Jeffries sang a holiday carol for the crowd. A blind pianist, Shep Thomas, accompanied her on a baby grand. An assistance dog curled at Shep's feet. Ah. She was home free.

Myrna broke the lyrics with a nod toward the pianist. "You play it, now, Shep." When Shep smiled back, the stage lights glinted on a gold-rimmed front tooth in his mouth. Smoothly, Myrna turned back to the crowd.

Hope hurried behind the business side of the counter. "Excuse me, Little Momma." She scooted sideways to get past a very pregnant young woman. Leanne King was just about as saucy a Southerner as she'd ever met in New York City. Then again, it couldn't be easy to be in Leanne's condition at only seventeen.

Leanne bussed a table into a large rubber tub. "What in green goobers are you doing back? Didn't you just finish your shift, like, half an hour ago?"

Hope reached for the heavy tub. "Yeah, but—"

Curiosity crept across Leanne's face. "Wait a sec. No, no, no, no, no. Weren't you going someplace with Ivan?"

Hope wrestled her emotions into a smirk. It was something of a challenge, given the catch in her throat. "Ivan and I...well, we're not so much anymore." Again, she reached for Leanne's tub of dirty dishes. "You shouldn't be lifting that. Gimme

26

now. Come on. Here." With that, Hope took the load from Leanne and headed back toward the kitchen, belting out in spot-on harmony with Myrna's continuing carol.

Leanne quickly snagged her, lowering her voice confidentially. "Hey, you're not gonna tell Frank you caught me snoozin' back there, are you?"

Hope stopped. She balanced the tub on the counter and leaned toward the girl confidentially. "No, but you can't keep that up. You've got no business, pushing eight months pregnant, sleeping on the cold, hard pantry floor."

"I leaned on those flour sacks. I put plastic on them. You do what you gotta do."

"You know, something tells me that the Health Department wouldn't be so down with that."

Earnestly, Leanne hung onto Hope's arm. "Please...please don't rat me out to Frank. I already got myself kicked out from that room I had. Last thing I can afford is to get booted from here, too."

Hope wrestled with the soft spot she had in her heart for Leanne. As snarky as the girl could get, she did respect her for carrying her baby all alone. Still, Frank would have a conniption if he ever happened upon her sleeping arrangements. "Okay, but you've gotta know, you can't keep stowing away in the pantry. You could get the place shut down. Then where'd we all be?"

"I got no place to go," Leanne pleaded.

"What about the women's shelter? You try that?"

Leanne peeked through the windowpane in the kitchen door. "What, are you kiddin' me? My folks probably have them looking for me all over those kinds of places. Anywhere there's a database."

"Would it be so bad if they found you?"

"Hope, how many times do I gotta tell you? I can't go home yet. Not till I pop this melon out of my pooch."

Everything in Hope wrangled over what to do. "Leanne. Sweetie—"

"They don't know, okay? And if there's any way I can work it, they never will."

Oh. Hope nodded. "You're giving up the baby."

Shame slouched across Leanne's face. "Course, I am. I have to. Then, I can go home."

"All right. Okay. Till that day comes, you're staying with me." Not waiting for an answer, Hope hoisted the tub and pushed through the swinging doors to the kitchen.

No sooner had Hope appeared than chief cook, Frank Abernathy, spotted her from the stove. "I thought you clocked out, Hope. You know I can't pay no double shifts."

Hope set the tub on the counter by the stainless sinks. "I'll still make plenty in tips, busy as you are."

Frank nodded. "Fine by me. Long as that's understood."

Leanne trudged up the stairs to Hope's third-floor brownstone apartment. What a day it had been. The building wasn't much to look at, what with the high price of living in Manhattan. Her feet sure were barking. They were like thirsty dogs, yapping at her with every step. "That elevator ever work?"

"Not to my knowledge." Hope fished out her keys. "I like to think of it as my own private stair machine. Think how much we're saving on a gym."

Panting, Leanne reached the landing. She took her nylon duffel bag off her shoulder.

Hope unlocked her unit. "You could have let me carry that for you."

Leanne rubbed her lower back. "Not like I got that much."

Hope swung the door open and gestured for Leanne to enter. "Be it ever so humble..." Hope snapped on the lights.

Leanne wandered inside. It was a pretty decent place. A potted red poinsettia was on the table, just like the kind her mom always put out in December. Handmade quilts were draped around, even on the futon she spotted in the spare room. Watercolors of country landscapes hung on the walls, signed with Hope's initials. It was actually kind of homey. "You paint?"

"Used to. Haven't in a while."

"Not too shabby, in an Old MacDonald, retro kind of way." Leanne peered through the door to Hope's spare room. "So, this is where I'll park it, back here?"

"My roommate, she's touring with a show for a couple more months. Pretty much garage sale chic in there, but—"

"No, no. It's great. Really great." Okay, maybe she'd overstated that. It wasn't great compared to her room at home, but it did look fairly awesome now. It was a far cry cleaner than the dump she'd been thrown out of, and it sure beat the stuffings out of the cold pantry floor of the Café Troubadour. This was definitely a place to stay, just as long as Hope would let her. She set her duffel bag down in the closet and followed Hope back into the living room. "I promise I won't be a bother."

"No bother," Hope replied. "Company might be nice, now that Ivan and I won't be seeing much of each other."

Leanne could relate. Boy, could she ever. She knew exactly what it was like to be deleted like somebody's unread spam. How it was that a guy could be so into her one minute, then onto someone else the next, she'd never understand. The bizarre thing was that Hope didn't seem all that upset, nothing like the blubberfest Leanne knew she'd been when she first hit town last summer. "Not to hack into your network, but was this your choice?"

"Yeah, but...it's complicated." Hope hung her coat and hat on a hook near the door.

Better not push it. Fine. Hope didn't want to talk about Ivan. Okie skimokie. Just because they'd be rooming together didn't mean they had to go all Truth or Dare besties with each other.

"You allergic to cats?"

Leanne scanned the apartment warily. "Uh...I dunno. Doubt it."

Hope shrugged. "Guess I should have asked you that before you climbed all of those stairs, but..." She checked around the wall to the kitchen. "Smokey! You gonna to show yourself?"

Apparently Hope's cat wasn't going to make an appearance.

Fine by me.

Hope turned back around. "Aloof little diva. But don't be surprised if she snuggles up to you at night. Has to be at her option, of course."

Just then, a small, charcoal-colored cat peered tentatively around the door to the spare room. Leanne reasoned that she should probably make nice. She took a tentative step in Smokey's direction.

"Take it slow," Hope advised. "She still has claws."

"I have a dog," Leanne mentioned. "Coco. At home and all." Leanne squatted down. Yow. Not the easiest thing to do in her condition. She brushed her fingers on the floor. Maybe Smokey would come to her.

Hope smiled, remembering. "We had dogs, too. Dogs and cats and horses and sheep and cows and goats and you name it."

Leanne peered up at Hope, surprised. "You lived out in the sticks?"

Hope nodded, her lips pressed together. There was a wistful flicker in her eyes. "Yeah, till I was about your age. I did."

three

By the light of a lantern, Charity cranked her father's freshly washed cotton shirt through their wringer. The fabric was wearing at the elbows, she noted. It would need to be patched.

Charity watched quietly as her father and grandfather busied themselves across the room, replacing a broken chair rung. As much furniture as they made and sold, theirs was always the last to get attention.

Opa smiled at her, a familiar twinkle in his eye. He nudged Dat. "Every time I look at her, I still see her mother."

"*Ja, ja,*" Dat agreed. "More all the time."

"Same hair, brown as mahogany, same fine bones, same pale blue eyes."

Charity lowered her gaze. Never would she begin to say such things of herself, but it warmed her to hear Opa say them to Dat. All these years, Dat had missed Mamm so. What a privilege it was to remind him of her.

Charity shook the wrinkles out of Dat's damp shirt. What a shame she couldn't remember Mamm better. Flashes of Mamm's face were sweet, but so very fleeting. Fainter still were echoes of Mamm's voice. Just when she thought she'd captured one, it drifted from her grasp.

Dat looked up again as he set the broken rung aside. "You need not do wash tonight."

Since his labors continued, why shouldn't hers? "One less thing in the morning. I want to get an early start to market."

A draft blew in as the door flung open. Aaron and Isaac hurried in, then latched the door for the night.

Dat looked up from the chair. "What kept you two so late? Your sister made a fine pot pie."

Isaac hung his hat. "We ate ourselves full at the Beachey's."

Dat nodded pleasantly. "Did you, now? It wonders me about what else went on there."

Aaron ambled into the room. "They showed us the milking machines they got."

Charity averted her gaze. Dat would be kind, but he would not like the sound of that.

"And what did you think, then?" Dat asked.

"Tell him, Isaac," Aaron prodded.

Isaac moved to his brother's side. Aaron gave his arm a nudge. "Tell him what you told me."

"Well... It's just..." Isaac scratched his head. "I was thinking on it awhile, how they got the electric milking machines approved."

"For business," Opa underscored.

"Right," Isaac hesitated.

Again, Aaron prodded his twin with a look.

"Okay, okay."

Dat dusted off his knees. "Aaron, let your brother decide what he will say, before he says it."

Isaac took a breath. "Think how much more furniture we could make. We'd have more to sell if we got some equipment like they use in the other districts. They have lathes and saws and sanders. The bishop said he'd allow it."

Charity watched as her father paused. He would have just the right response for her brothers.

"Tell me, Isaac. What message did Opa share with all of us, last Sunday meeting? Aaron, you may answer. If you call it to mind."

Aaron looked completely stumped.

Isaac's head drooped. "Not everything that is permitted is best."

"*Sehr gut*, Isaac. So, you were listening."

"*Ja*, Dat. And Opa. I heard."

Dat put his hand on Isaac's shoulder. "There are many things that other people do that we choose not to do. Even other Amish. Hear me that I do not fault you for asking." Dat glanced between the two of them. "Your Rumspringa years will come to an end, now-once. You will both have to decide these things for yourselves yet. Even Gott will not take that choice from you. But until that time, as long as you live under this roof, this is my decision. We have made fine furniture without English electricity for many generations in this family. We will continue to do that. Do you understand?"

Isaac nodded. Dat turned to Aaron. Aaron accepted it, too. The two of them headed up the stairs to their room. It was over.

Charity picked up her father's jacket. She fished through its pockets, emptying them in preparation for washing.

Dat cast a glance her way. "Daughter, tell me. Do you dislike Daniel?"

The question was startling, so out of the blue. "Dislike him? Not at all. I just have work to do." She pulled a sealed envelope from the pocket of Dat's jacket, her mind awhirl. It was just like Dat to pick up mail and on his way back from town, and then forget it was in his pocket. Just not on washday.

As her grandfather steadied the chair legs, her father edged the new rung into place with a mallet. "You might take some time for yourself, like the others do. I want you to be happy."

"I am happy, Dat. I hardly need to run around to know where I belong." Charity glanced at the envelope she held in her hand. It was forest green in color, like the holly along the edge of their woods. The envelope felt stiff, as if it contained a card. Above the New York City return address was a woman's name:

Hope Bright.

Charity looked up, as stunned as she was curious. Never had she known of another woman in their family, not since her grandmother died. "Who is Hope?"

Opa clouded with concern, but Dat maintained his usual composure. He busied himself righting the chair. "No one to us, Child."

Charity examined the envelope, puzzled. As reluctant as she was to challenge Dat, something about it prickled her inside. "But her last name is Bright, like ours."

Dat wordlessly crossed to her and held out his hand. "Trust me, Charity. You were not meant to see this. And you would best forget that you did."

Everything inside Charity begged. Pursue it. "But Dat..."

His voice was gentle, yet firm. "*Guten nacht*, Charity."

Dat asked very little of her. So, when he did, she felt more than obliged to obey. She relinquished the envelope to him. Wistfully, she watched as he left the room. "*Guten nacht*, Dat."

Charity's gaze turned to Opa as he put his woodworking tools away for the night. There had been no mistaking the recognition she'd seen in his eyes. "Is she anything to you, Opa?"

Her grandfather contemplated the question for a while, a long-buried pain resurfacing on his face. "Some things are best unsaid."

"Then she is," Charity supposed.

Regret etched across Opa's expression. "She was."

As tired as she'd been from the long day's work, Charity slept very little that night. Hour after hour passed. She did everything she knew to coax her eyes to stay shut. Maybe rolling over would help. It didn't.

She really should take advantage of the time she had left. Dat always said he needed to "sleep two rows at a time" to make up for restless nights like this. How in the world could she actually do that, any more than a farmer could plow two rows at once? Try as she might to nod off, nothing stopped her curious mind from stirring.

It was unsettling to realize that the Bright family tree extended beyond what she had supposed. All of her life, she'd hung the sole black bonnet on the rack by the door, beside the four black hats of her father, grandfather, and brothers. Who was this Hope—a woman with their last name—living outside in the English world?

Finally, the night ended. Most of it, anyway. And just like that, Charity was twenty. She rested a hand against her throat. She would make nothing of this milestone. Yet, she knew. A great and ominous divide had been crossed, and there would be no return.

Before the sun, Charity rose. She put on a clean dress and apron, then twisted her waist-length tresses into a neat bun at the back of her head. *Careful*, she reminded herself as she situated her mother's starched white kapp into place. She would make this memento last.

Charity had loaded her goods into the family buggy many times while Dat bridled the horse. It was their regular routine. But something about this morning felt different, in ways she could not describe. It wasn't her place to question her father, but rather to trust his wisdom about whatever had happened within their family.

It wasn't a blind faith she had in him. It had been tried and tested over the years growing up in his devoutly run household. Still, she couldn't help hoping that he would answer the many questions that tugged at her mind.

Stroking their horse's mane, Dat finally spoke. "I could take this load in myself, you know. It is, after all, your birthday. You could stay. You could be here to receive Daniel."

Whatever did he mean by that? Had Daniel said something? Shyness swept over her. She dropped her gaze. "You like him for me."

"Daniel is a fine young man. You would be wise to notice."

She couldn't prevent a slight smile from curling. "I have noticed."

Her father moved toward the buggy. "You keep your secrets well."

"Like you, Dat."

For a moment, her father stopped, clearly conflicted. "She was my sister."

Charity took the truth in, quietly stunned. "You have a sister? I have an aunt?" It was so strange to even say those words.

The cloud that crossed Dat's face was nothing short of grief. Charity watched him, transfixed. He expelled a heavy sigh. "You are twenty today. I suppose you are old enough to know, now. I had a younger sister," he allowed. "Once. But no longer. It was her choice."

Charity felt her eyes mist. Quickly, she blinked. What if Dat noticed? He might think her less mature than she wanted to appear. "She was shunned?"

Faintly, Dat acknowledged the hard truth. "It was after your Mamm died. Hope was about your age then. You were only three. Next to me, your mother was her dearest friend, and she... Well, she never got over Grace dying that way." Dat stared into the distance. "So, she left. She had already been baptized, but she said she had rushed into it too young. She wanted to go back and start her Rumspringa again, as if she had never ended it."

Inwardly, Charity grappled for understanding. "Go back out?" Many enjoyed Rumspringa into their early twenties. But the idea of going back to resume Rumspringa after being baptized Amish—that was entirely new. "Is that ever done?"

Dat shook his head. "Not with the blessing of the church, not after baptism. That is for sure and certain." Dat's eyes dropped. "She was devastated over Grace. So ferhuddled, doncha know. She wanted to turn back time. Make her choices all over again. It always wondered me if she called it what she did because, deep inside, she knew she would want to come home, when she was a bit older."

Quietly, something burned in Charity's heart. "Do you still think there's a chance? Maybe she still misses us."

"*Ja*, I never doubt that she does. When she left, she said she could hardly stand to part with you and your baby brothers, even for a day. But there was this faraway look in her eye and..." Dat slouched. "Seventeen years, now. And she never came back."

Charity studied her father intently. "But she writes to you."

"Every Christmas."

"What does she say?"

Dat moved toward the barn door. "I return the cards unopened, but not before many prayers."

It was Charity's turn to exercise restraint. She knew her father to be a man of deep communion with Gott.

"Perhaps it seems harsh," he went on, "but she does know where and how we live. If shunning draws her home yet, then it is not rejection. Not at all, Charity. It is the deepest kind of love."

Dat guided the horse and buggy toward the market where they sold their wares. A small boy pointed them out to his mother as they crossed the busy street. The mother urged her son onward, but he still continued to stare. Even in small town traffic, they stood out so. Charity was accustomed to the attention they always drew among the English. As humbly as they went about their business, there were always plenty of gawks and whispers, not only from the town folk, but also from visiting tourists.

Being the center of attention wasn't something Charity relished. Plus, with so many cell phones out there, almost all the English had some kind of a camera now. Politely dodging their photographs was more challenging than ever.

Why was it that people found their simple ways to be such a curiosity? If the English world was so fascinating, why did tourists take such an interest in them? Going to town was like living in a fishbowl, complete with wide-eyed faces, tapping insistently at the glass.

Charity glanced sidelong at her father, silently contemplating, as he guided their horse into town.

An affectionate arc bordered her father's lips. "Your mother used to do that very thing, so she did."

Charity broke her gaze. "What?"

"Think so loudly that I could not help but hear."

How did he always catch her? She masked her amusement. "Forgive me."

Her father adjusted the reins. "For putting to mind your dear Mamm? No need for forgiveness. No, I thank you."

As much as Dat still loved her mother, he wasn't one to raise the subject of her so very often.

He was giving her an opportunity. "You still miss her?"

"Every day Gott blesses me to wake yet."

In the privacy of her heart, Charity said a prayer of thanks. As she'd ridden along to town that very morning, she'd made one humble request for her birthday: that another opening would be provided to talk more about what Dat had briefly shared with her that morning. Cautiously, Charity tested the waters. "That must have been so hard. Losing your wife and your sister, all at once."

He guided the carriage toward a storefront with a place to tie up the horse. There were fewer and fewer of those these days. "I try to mind what I still have. You and the boys. Your Opa after all these years."

As he parked the buggy, Charity gathered her courage. During the night, an idea had come to her. It was the reason she'd scarcely been able to fall back to sleep. She squeezed the seat to her side, trying to maintain at least the appearance of being calm. "Dat, what if I returned her card this year?"

A few seconds passed as Dat considered it. "Now that you know, I suppose you could take it to the post office to send back to her."

"No, I mean..." Charity reminded herself to think before she spoke. Dat would appreciate that. Assurance was what he'd need to hear. She would lead off with it. "You know that I want to be baptized, to commit to remain Amish for life. You also know I'm still of age for Rumspringa before I do." She took a breath. "What if—instead of just staying at home like most do—what if I went into the world on Rumspringa? What if I used that time to return the card to her in New York City myself?"

Dat drew back. "In person? No. The church would never permit it."

Charity paused. *Be respectful.* "Do you mean the church would never permit it or you?"

Dat ran his hand through his beard. He always did that when he was deep in thought.

"Opa is a minister," she continued. "I doubt that Bethany's Uncle Caleb would resist the idea. Perhaps they could persuade the bishop."

He rested his hand on his chin. "Even if the bishop would allow it, what good would it do?"

"Maybe I could bring her home."

"Maybe she would convince you to stay."

Though she rarely did it, Charity reflexively laid her hand on his shoulder. "Dat, trust me. I could never leave my family, my faith. You and Opa, the boys—you are my life."

How long the silence was that followed, Charity wasn't sure. He must be considering it. Surely, he was. She watched as he scanned the modern world surrounding their buggy, a sober expression forming.

Finally, he turned to her. He stroked her bonnet affectionately and looked full into her face. "This world is surely not without its allures, Charity. You would do best not to underestimate it."

four

Charity stooped to help Bethany gather collards from the Hooley's vegetable garden. The dark green leaves would be far sweeter now that the first frost had passed. It would take a lot of collards to feed the many who had come to the aid of the Hooleys that day. It was hard work but, at the same time, very satisfying to think how much everyone would enjoy what they prepared.

She gazed across the yard to the building project in process. Dozens of neighboring men had joined her father, grandfather, and brothers to help add on a *dawdi haus* for the Hooley's ageing parents. The structure was modestly sized—just a bedroom with a small living area—but the addition to the main house would meet their needs well.

It was just one of the things that Charity loved about her community. When one family or another had any sort of need, the others would readily gather around to help. The womenfolk were there in force, too, preparing a tasty lunch of sandwiches and German potato salad for all of the workers. The collards they were picking would be steamed to round out the meal.

Out of the corner of her eye, Charity couldn't resist watching Daniel. He was assisting her father, framing a two-by-four into place. What a hard worker Daniel was. So strong and capable. All morning, he'd been laboring at Dat's side. She had no idea of what conversation might have passed between them, but something sang inside her, just at the sight of them together.

Bethany sidled up to Charity. "You realize you're staring."

Charity turned. "I was just—"

"He must really want to please your Dat."

Charity smiled as she flattened collard leaves into her basket. "Do you think we could change the subject?"

"All right. No problem. So, you really had an aunt who was shunned?"

Charity checked the attentions of the nearby women. "Shhh! They might hear."

Bethany moved closer. She lowered her voice to a whisper. "What happened? What is she like?"

"I wish I had thought to ask." Charity glanced around. Indeed, Esther Burkholder appeared to be eavesdropping as she harvested parsnips nearby in the garden. Discreetly, Charity tipped her bonnet toward Esther.

Bethany nodded. She was well accustomed to Charity's signals.

One challenge that knowing everyone in the community presented was keeping private things truly private. With Esther, it was easy to understand. She was a widow and probably just curious. Charity turned to face the woman. "Will this be enough of the collards, Esther?"

Esther checked over their baskets. "I suppose."

Charity led Bethany back toward the others.

Bethany leaned in close. "Esther is older. She would have known her."

"Bethany Beachey," Charity teased. "Are you saying I should engage in gossip?"

Bethany grinned. "Do you know that, in the English world, there are people who make their entire living on gossip? They call them gossip columnists. I read their stories in the newspapers when I was away last summer."

Bethany's Rumspringa years certainly had taken her far beyond their borders. It was another way she differed from most of the others their age. She'd taken a bus all the way to the Florida settlement where others in the Beachey family still lived. Charity knew better than to chatter too much with Bethany about her travels. It wasn't disinterest, not at all. But one minute they'd be talking about Bethany's adventures, and the next she'd be trying to explain all over again why she'd never chosen to take advantage of Rumspringa herself.

Why it was that her Aunt Hope had never returned, Charity didn't know. But maybe something in Bethany's experience could help. "Was it ever hard for you, when you traveled, to come back?"

Bethany's eyes widened. She leaned closer. "What... Are you thinking of going somewhere?"

Charity checked to be sure they weren't being overheard. Esther was at a safe distance. "Maybe, but... Was it hard?"

Bethany shrugged lightly. "Not really. I thought it might be, but in the end...this is my home. And you are here. I could never leave you."

Charity tapped Bethany's arm playfully. "You just wanted to rush back and catch that handsome Levi Hooley's eye."

Bethany's expression drooped. She glanced over at Levi where he worked with the men. "Hannah told me he called on her last night. She was elated."

Disappointed, Charity stopped. "Your own cousin... She never knew?"

Tears brimmed as Bethany shook her head. "I never told anyone but you. I guess you were right. It wasn't about the changes."

"Bethany... Oh, I am so sorry. I know you've had your hopes up about him for such a long time."

"Sometimes, I wonder," Bethany sighed. "They always talk to us about the virtues of being Plain, but...maybe I'm too plain."

Charity took hold of Bethany's shoulders and regarded her squarely. "Look at me, Bethany." She waited till Bethany tipped her chin up and returned her gaze. Bethany's reddening complexion made Charity ache, all the way to the pit of her stomach. Why had she brought Levi's name up at all?

Bethany ran a hand over her face, brushing the wetness away.

"Look at me and know that I will always tell you the truth." Charity felt her own eyes filling. "Bethany, you have the most beautiful heart of any woman I know. You are clever and delightful and, in every important way, truly exquisite. One day, I promise you—the right man—he will see that."

Leanne groaned. It figured that Hope's absentee roommate would have one of those clock radio alarms, the kind that were practically impossible to figure out how to mute. The pre-dawn D.J. needed to dial it back, too. For a New Yorker, the guy was maddeningly perky.

No one had ever accused Leanne of being a morning person. All during her growing up years, coaxing herself to push aside the warm covers and crawl out of bed had always been something of a battle. Now that she was sleeping for two, it was that much worse. First, there was that ever so delightful impulse to hurl just as soon as the day dawned. Next came the random kidney kicking. Had to be a boy. No girl could punt like that.

The bigger she'd gotten, the harder it was to get comfortable enough to sleep a wink at all. No matter which way she turned, something ached. There was no shutting her mind down either. It kept reminding her how little time she had left to sleep. Yeah, that helped. Then—wouldn't you know it—just after she'd finally managed to nod off, there was Dobie D.J., squawking his cock-a-doodle-doos.

Her parents were always up with the birds. That was a gene she sure hadn't gotten. She missed them something awful. No point thinking about that. She stared at her phone, then back up at the ceiling. No way she could face them. Not with her belly the size of a hot air balloon.

Shame pummeled her. She tossed it away, but it came flying right back, like a boomerang. It taunted her constantly with its na-na-nas, calling her every ugly name in the book. The only way to shut it up was to sleep. As if that ever happened. Truth be told, she'd hardly slept at all the night before on the Café Troubadour's freezing cold pantry floor. She closed her eyes again. At least she could soak in the warmth of the quilt and the softness of the pillow. Even the futon wasn't half bad.

A knock sounded at the door. That had to be Hope.

Moan.

Hope knocked again, this time a little louder. "Are you up?"

Leanne relished a last moment of comfort before throwing the covers back. "Not exactly, but I'm getting there."

Hope's voice carried through the door. "There's a terry robe of mine in the closet you can borrow."

"Thanks. Like it'll fit over this spare tire I've got goin'." As much as her lower back smarted, Leanne forced herself to sit up. She yawned groggily, and then rose to her swollen feet. The apartment smelled of fresh-brewed coffee, no doubt the caffeinated kind that she wasn't supposed to drink. Nothing about having this kid was easy. Absolutely nothing.

Leanne opened the door and shuffled into the kitchen. Hope was already up and dressed, hustling about, a whirlwind of energy, despite the early hour. It wasn't easy to know how to behave in someone else's home, but Hope seemed to make nothing of it. Maybe she shouldn't either.

Before Leanne even had time to mention her growling stomach, Hope flung open the refrigerator door and pulled out a pitcher of orange juice. "I know you're eating for two, Leanne, so help yourself to whatever you want," she offered. "Although that cream cheese in there is kind of dicey. Fine line between cheese and all out fungus, you know? I should toss that." Hope reached in and grabbed the cream cheese. She left the door open for Leanne.

Amidst the dairy, produce, and juices, Leanne spotted a gallon pickle jar, three quarters filled with coins. "That's where you keep your tips?"

Hope took a swallow of coffee. "Cold, hard cash. It's not like I can go to the bank every day, so I just toss it in there till it's full. I figure anybody who's desperate enough to forage for food while they're robbing me needs it way more than I do."

Leanne poured herself a glass of juice. It was hard not to envy Hope. For starters, Hope wasn't pregnant. She was also kind of pretty. Hope had one of those annoyingly sunny personalities. She really could light up a room. With her talent, she probably filled that pickle jar to bursting with change every single week. "Wish I could sing like you," Leanne muttered. "Then maybe Frank would let me wait tables, make some tips of my own. Can't hardly keep up, with what he pays me to wash dishes."

"Speaking of which, aren't you coming?"

Leanne leaned against the counter wearily as Hope rinsed her coffee cup. "Maybe I should call in sick."

Concern crossed Hope's face. "Are you?"

Leanne returned a chagrinned grimace. "Sick of being preggers. And I got five, six weeks left to go. Guess I should motivate."

Hope grabbed her keys and headed toward the front door. "All righty. See you there."

Leanne took a sip of juice. "Buy me some time with Frank, will ya?"

"I'll try. Lock up, okay?"

"Okay."

Hope hurried out and shut the door. But for Hope's illusive cat, Smokey, who hadn't yet made an appearance, Leanne found herself alone. Again.

Flying solo was definitely the worst part of being pregnant. Sure, the baby was moving around inside her, but that did little to cut through the loneliness that running away to New York City had caused. She had a bazillion virtual friends on her networking sites, but she'd known better than to give herself away by contacting any of her actual friends or relatives. She told herself that, soon enough, she'd be out of this mountain of a mess. She'd be able to take the bus home, as if it had never happened.

Leanne opened up the refrigerator again and surveyed its contents. Cooking eggs seemed like too much work, but a bag of bagels caught her eye. They were the cinnamon-raisin kind, like her mom always used to buy.

As she reached for the bag, Leanne took another gander at all the coins in Hope's pickle jar. Judging from the high concentration of quarters, she figured there had to be hundreds of dollars in there. *What I couldn't do with all that money.* Guilt grabbed her by the tonsils. Hope had been so nice to her, the last thing she should ever let even enter her mind was touching a red cent of that money. Still, in the secrecy of her thoughts, she had to admit that it was tempting.

Charity bore down to unscrew the lid from a canning jar. It was rusty and would need to be replaced, but the glass jar could be used again. Putting up preserves was an everyday job this time of year, so it was always nice to have Bethany there to help. Beyond the fruit to be peeled and processed, there were always the jars to be sterilized, filled, and labeled for market.

As Charity checked the seal on their cooling preserves, she also kept an eye outside her kitchen window. Aaron and Isaac were in the yard, dutifully chopping and stacking hewn wood, but it was her father's and grandfather's return in their buggy that made her so restless. She'd hardly been able to think of another thing since they'd left to take her question before the church leadership. Now, here they were, back again.

They would likely have a decision.

Bethany joined her at the window. "How does he look to you?"

Charity strained to interpret the expression on Dat's face, even while he was still at a distance outside. "Hard to tell." There were times she was so thankful for her brothers, and this was one of them. "Good. They're helping Dat with the buggy. He's coming this way."

As her father headed toward the house, Charity turned to Bethany. "He has an answer. He must. Bethany, you know I dearly love your company, but will you please go for a little while? He'll only tell me in private."

Bethany wiped her hands. "But then you have to promise you'll tell me."

Charity brushed Bethany's shoulder. "Every word."

Satisfied, Bethany snatched a stack of jar labels, stuck them into her pocket and headed for the door. She reached it just as Dat swung it open.

Dat removed his hat and hung it on its peg by the entry. "Leaving so early in the day, Bethany?"

Bethany snatched her bonnet and tied her cape loosely at her throat. "To get more labels. I should have thought to bring more." In a moment, Bethany was gone. She closed the door behind herself, leaving Charity alone with her father.

Everything in Charity wanted burst with the question. What had happened? She focused her attention on her work as Dat took off his coat and hung it. It would not serve her to rush him.

Finally, he turned. He approached the kitchen counter where she was working. "I suppose you would like to know what was said."

She rubbed her hands dry on her apron. "I would."

Nathan pulled out a chair for her. "Sit down, Daughter."

Obediently, Charity took a seat across from her father. He remained silent for a while, a thoughtful expression in his eyes.

"There was no small discussion," he started. "There are those, like your grandfather and me. We have our fears yet. But the church has no restrictions about what a young person is allowed to do on Rumspringa. Even if it comes to sin." Dat laced his fingers loosely and rested them on the table. "The bishop said that putting up boundaries conflicts with what Rumspringa is about. True enough, most stay here for singings and such. It is not encouraged, but still, he said that if a young person wants to go out among the Englishers for a while, no one should get in the way. Then, a free choice can be made between the English way of life and ours."

Charity measured her words. "So there would be no limits, even when it comes to traveling to see a shunned person, out in the English world."

Thoughtfully, her father sat back. "Caleb Beachey had a mind for that."

"And Opa?"

Dat paused, his brow lightly knitted. "We Amish shun many things the English world accepts, things we pray you will not choose, even when you have the chance."

Charity searched Dat's face. "And so...?"

He ran his fingers through his graying beard. "So, they have left it to me."

"I see." Never once had Charity known Dat to go against the most conservative suggestions of their leadership. What she hadn't expected was that they would have put the decision back into his lap. Something in her hesitated. Should she inquire further? She straightened in her seat and gathered her resolve. "Have you made a decision?"

Dat's chest filled and emptied. Like always, his face exuded authority. "I have two conditions for you. There is no time that my sister misses us like Christmas. That is when you would be most likely to get her to come back with you, now-once. If I give you my blessing to go, would you promise to be home by Christmas?"

Charity heart skipped a beat. "Oh, Dat... I could never miss Christmas with you. I could be back in time to make Christmas dinner, with Aunt Hope here to help me."

Dat's face still looked so sober. "*Ja*, well... I pray that she will. Now, I am also concerned that you not go alone. The city is a dangerous place."

She could scarcely believe it. He was going to let her go. She couldn't help bubbling over. "Bethany would come. She's still on Rumspringa. She's seen the city. We could ride the train together."

Her father raised a patient hand. "I know that Bethany is your dearest friend, but I am of a mind that you go with someone else."

"Oh?"

"I have spoken to Daniel."

Charity felt her mouth drop. She put a hand to her upturned lips. "Daniel. Is he willing?"

Dat nodded, a hint of a smile forming. "If you are."

Once Dat made a decision, he was not one to dawdle about setting matters into motion. As Charity cleaned up from lunch, she watched outside the kitchen window. Indeed, Dat had gotten her brothers to help him bring the horse and buggy out from the barn once again. He strode across the yard toward the house.

Dat didn't make much of things. He didn't announce his plans in advance. That wasn't his nature. He simply opened the kitchen door and asked her to put on her cape and bonnet. They would be going into town, that very afternoon, to make arrangements for her trip.

Little was said as they traversed the road into town. Her father preferred it that way. In a way, she did, too. It gave her time to think and pray about all that was unfolding.

A car horn tooted twice from behind them. Jarred, Charity craned around to check. "I suppose they want to pass."

Dat held his ground. "We give way to the Englishers in their world. They should do as much in ours." A few seconds later, he guided their buggy off to the right. Dat was like that. He'd say something, and then in time, he'd think better of it. It was one of the things she admired about him.

Charity watched in silence as the automobile zoomed past. A boy in the rear seat turned back and waved. Before she knew it he had raised a camera. Instinctively, she drew up her apron to cover her face till the car was well out of sight. The challenges of venturing into the English world were always there. She would have to be prepared.

Before Charity knew it, they were seated across from a travel agent in town. She tried her best not to stare. Still, there were some things she couldn't help but notice. The woman's hair was bobbed quite short, framing darkly painted eyes. Burgundy lipstick encircled impossibly white teeth. Freshly polished nails danced across the computer keyboard, clicking with every stroke. Charity took it all in, then reminded herself not to judge the woman. Like a cool breeze, a thought wafted over her. *Was this what her Aunt Hope would look like after so many years in the city?*

Dat did most of the talking. He bought two roundtrip train tickets to New York City's Penn Station. Charity's eyes widened when he scheduled their departure for the third of December.

Tomorrow.

In the morning, she'd get on the first train with Daniel. There would be twenty-one days—three full weeks to persuade her Aunt Hope to return home with them on Christmas Eve.

What an adventure was ahead of her. Never in her life had she known anyone in her family to take the train or even to visit the station. Trains were a modern-day convenience they'd never had need of before. But it was a very long way to New York City, much farther than could be managed by horse and buggy.

Under his breath, Dat counted as he laid out cash to cover the charges.

The agent rose and excused herself to get a receipt.

Gratitude swelled in Charity. "Such a nice, long trip, Dat. Can you manage without me so long?"

Dat eased back into his chair. "When a tree has sunken its roots deep into a place, it cannot be uprooted overnight. The soil must be watered. It must be loosened, ever so gently, doncha know. That will take every bit of this time."

When the next day dawned, Bethany joined the Bright family on the train platform to see Charity and Daniel off for their trip. Bethany seemed almost as excited about it as she was. It was far from Charity's purpose to explore the world. That might be what Rumspringa was about for Bethany, but not for Charity. What that flutter in her heart was, she wasn't sure. Maybe it was about going on this journey with Daniel. Maybe it was the thought that, soon, she would meet her Aunt Hope. Maybe it was both.

Charity turned to her twin brothers. "Can you survive Dat's cooking for a few weeks?"

Aaron feigned distress. "If I have to."

"You could always learn yourselves," Charity teased.

"Just come home soon," Isaac added.

Bethany squeezed Charity tight, whispering, with an eye toward Daniel. "What I would not give to be in your place. But still, I am so happy for you. Promise to remember every tiny detail for me?"

Charity grasped Bethany's hands in hers. "Everything," she promised. As she approached, Charity couldn't help but overhear the words that passed between Daniel and her father.

"You will bring her home to me safely," Dat said. "By the twenty-fourth."

Daniel nodded. "You have my word."

Charity turned to Opa. It was easy to tell that, of all the family, her grandfather was the most uncomfortable in this contemporary setting. Though a few of their Old Order had slowly begun to embrace certain aspects of modern life, he stood firmly with Dat in support of the overwhelmingly conservative majority. She embraced him lovingly. "*Aufweidersehen*, Opa."

"I am not sure this is wise," he murmured.

Charity gazed into his troubled face. "Then pray for me, Opa. Pray that I will be strong."

"I will," he assured. "I will not stop until I meet you here again."

Charity's eyes filled as she turned to her father. "Dat..."

With a soft smile, he took Aunt Hope's unopened Christmas card from his coat pocket and handed it to Charity.

She glanced at the card, and then kissed his cheek. "Thank you for trusting me with this. This is such a gift to me, Dat, but I hope it will end up being a gift to us all."

Dat nodded, his eyes intent. He took her in his arms. "Gott go with you."

A final boarding call sounded. The time had come. Charity and Daniel hurried toward the train. No sooner than they had stowed their bags and taken their seats, the doors closed and the train began to pull away.

From her window, Charity could see them all. Bethany waved furiously. Aaron and Isaac were rapt at the wonder of the train. Dat stood straight, but for a consoling arm that he draped across Opa's shoulders. It seemed that Opa was more than a little concerned to see her go. Deep in her heart, Charity made a promise. She would allay their fears. Soon, she would return to them, once and for all.

five

The strains of a Yuletide noel resounded within Manhattan's Café Troubadour. Hope's alto rang out in counterpoint to Myrna's soulful mezzo-soprano.

"I heard the bells on Christmas Day
Their old familiar carols play,
And wild and sweet,
The words repeat,
Of peace on earth, good will to men..."

Seated at the piano on the café's stage, Shep accompanied Myrna and Hope, his assistance dog curled at his feet. Shep never ceased to amaze Hope. What a wonder it was that, though blind all of his life, Shep's fingers found their way across the keys with such artistry.

As they finished the carol, a smattering of diners applauded. She had to admit it. That always felt good. Shep segued into a holiday medley. Hope gave his shoulders an appreciative squeeze.

Myrna clicked off the microphone, and turned to Shep. "Thanks, Baby Doll."

Continuing to play, Shep grinned widely. "You two just make me sound good."

As they stepped off the stage, Hope took Myrna's arm and led her aside, into the ladies' locker room. Calling it a locker room might have been overstating the case. It was more like an employees' restroom with some tall metal cabinets set inside.

Hope opened her locker. She could only pray that the pseudo-lemony scent of industrial-strength bathroom disinfectant hadn't completely permeated the dress she'd brought. "You got this for an hour or so?"

A knowing twinkle lit in Myrna's eyes. "Sure. You tell Mr. Fancy Pants Broadway Director that if he don't hire you, he's got me to reckon with."

"Should set me apart." Hope untied her apron. There was always something about putting on the right clothes that helped Hope start to feel less like a waitress and more like the character.

Myrna reached for Hope's uniform. "Lemme hang all this."

That was Myrna. Always eager to help. In a flash, Hope's uniform was stowed. She slipped the soft red chemise over her head, then pulled her hair down from its chignon. She fluffed it loosely around her shoulders and checked her lipstick in the mirror. What a great opportunity this was. It was amazing that her agent had even gotten her the call.

Myrna took a step back. "Look at you, Girl. Mmm!"

"You think?" Hope kicked off her comfy-soled waitress shoes and replaced them with a stylish little pair of black flats. The transformation complete, she headed for the door.

Myrna followed. She squeezed Hope's arm as they walked back through to the restaurant's service floor. "Shoulders back, Baby. He won't even know what hit him once you step up!"

Café regular "Goldie" Goldstone grumbled to Hope as she passed. "Are we completely forgetting about my double mocha decaf latte with whipped?" The man was as gaudily attired as he was cynical. A greased comb-over failed to cover the bald spot at his crown.

Myrna stepped to Goldie's side. "Now, you tell me why you can't stomach one morning with me making it for you." Myrna motioned to Hope. "Go on, break a leg, Honey. I'll take care of Goldie."

Sourly scanning his paper, Goldie retorted to Myrna, loud enough for Hope to hear. "And exactly what makes her think this will be different from the last hundred-fifty failed auditions?"

Myrna patted Goldie on his high-maintenance back. "Christmas is coming, Goldie. Have a little faith."

Relieved, Hope blew Myrna a grateful kiss and sailed out of the door.

Charity drank in the passing scenery. The train glided along the tracks to New York smoothly, much more so than she'd anticipated. Sometimes, it didn't seem like the train itself was moving at all, only the ever-changing landscape.

Daniel sat engrossed, studying the map of Manhattan the travel agent had provided. He wanted to make sure he knew exactly where they were going, she supposed. Already, he'd found where the train would let them off at Penn Station. He'd also located the address of Aunt Hope's apartment, just a mile's walk away. Charity was glad they'd be able to get around the city on foot. Trains were one thing. Cars and subways, she could do without.

Charity watched Daniel as he jotted down directions from the map. He really was taking the responsibility of escorting her to the city seriously. He also seemed to be enjoying it, at least so far. Never had they spent so much time together, not by themselves.

For a while, Charity tried to think of what she might say to him, but in time she relaxed into quiet fascination at their surroundings. It wasn't just the change from the gently rolling hills of Pennsylvania to the looming skyscrapers of Manhattan that set Charity's mind to thinking. It was the people and the way that, the closer they got to Penn Station, the more crowded and moody their train car became.

With every passing stop, Charity observed each person, young and old, who boarded. Trips to the market on the outskirts of town had done little to prepare her for so many different walks of life. Actually, though she did her best to be discreet, she couldn't help but notice the stares that she, herself, drew. Reflexively, she straightened the ribbons of her kapp.

Daniel leaned over toward Charity. He lowered his voice. "Don't let them make you feel self-conscious."

Charity dropped her eyes. How was it that he'd known what she'd been thinking? "No, it's just... Perhaps without my Mamm's kapp I would draw less attention."

Daniel smiled at her admiringly. "It's not the covering that makes them stare, Charity. You are quite beautiful."

Charity blushed. Never had she heard such a compliment. How should she respond to him? To accept his words felt prideful, but to discount them seemed unappreciative. Finally, she opted to just change the subject. "New York City must be such an expensive place to live alone. I wonder if my Aunt Hope got married...or has children."

"Her name is still Bright on the envelope."

"I hear some don't take a married name."

Daniel raised his brow thoughtfully. "Well, if she is married or has a family, getting her to come home could be that much more of a challenge."

"They could all come."

"They could," he supposed. "But would they?"

Charity bolstered her resolve. "She writes every Christmas because something in her still wants to come home. We have to believe that."

As she emerged from the busy train station with Daniel, Charity's chest tightened. Car horns blared. Men with shrill whistles hailed taxis. Widespread pedestrian traffic contributed to the cacophony. It was unlike anything she'd ever seen or heard.

A raggedly dressed woman pushed a shopping cart toward them. It was filled to the brim with all kinds of things. The woman passed by, raging at an unseen foe. "You shut up! Shut your hideous mouth. You just talk, talk, talk, and you think for a second anybody's listening to you?"

Charity slowed. She looked back briefly, but Daniel kept walking them forward. It seemed impossible to take it all in all at once. The sights, the sounds, the smells... Sensory overload, really. She had heard about what life was like in the city, but nothing had prepared her for the reality before her. Neon lights glowed, even though the sun was still shining. Glitzy decorations were in storefront after storefront. There were men dressed as Santa, plastic reindeer, and sparkling Christmas balls the size of hay bales. What she didn't see was a sign of anything that had any connection with what Christmas was really all about. At least to them.

Daniel checked over at her as they waited at a crosswalk. Again, she offered to carry her own bag. Once again, he declined.

"You all right?" he asked.

Charity turned to him. "Yes. It's just a lot, much more than I had imagined.

Leanne exited the security door of Hope's building. Wouldn't you know it? She was just in time to find Hope's old boyfriend, Ivan, there ringing the bell.

What was he doing there? Hope said they were over. She shut the door protectively. "She's not home, Ivan. You know she works. I gotta go, too."

"I thought with her audition she might—"

Leanne rolled her eyes. What did he want from her? "So, go to the theater. Maybe you can catch her leavin'. Anyway, I was under the impression that you two were kind of kaputski."

A lovelorn look crossed Ivan's face. "Is that what she said?"

Leanne glanced at her watch. How had the entire morning gotten away from her? "Look, I'm already late and Frank gets way cranky about that. Maybe you should take this up with someone who gives a rip."

She blew by him to descend the stairs. That's when she saw them. At the bottom of the steps stood a young couple seriously in need of an extreme makeover. Though they didn't appear to be much older than she was, the way they were dressed, they might as well have been from another century. Come to think of it, the girl looked a little like one of those people at the airport who was always asking for money.

The guy spoke. "Hello. I'm Daniel. I'm with, uh...Charity, here—"

Leanne threw up her hands as she descended the stairs. She put on her best foreign accent. "No charity. No speak-a de Eng-leesh."

"Excuse me, Miss," the young woman said. "Could you please—"

Leanne blew out an exasperated breath. She opened her coat to display her protruding belly. "Sorry, but do I look like I've got somethin' here to donate?"

"No, no, we're not collecting," she explained. "My name is Charity. I believe my Aunt Hope lives in this building." Charity checked the green envelope in her hand. "Yes. This is the address. Do you know Hope Bright?"

Hope shook out her hands. Was it all a dream, or was she really standing in the wings of a bona fide Broadway theater? The musty scent of countless past productions filled her head. And the curtain—that alone was magnificent.

Would it be too geeky to touch it? She checked around. Good. No one was watching. She reached to her side and ran the back of her hand across the plush velvet.

How on earth could she be perspiring, as drafty as it was? There was nowhere to put her coat, so she draped it over her arm.

Should she go over the lines once more? No need. She had those words down cold. Lines were not her problem. It was the pounding heart that threatened to jump right out of her chest.

She closed her eyes. *Please, help me do my best work.*

As the prior auditionee finished, Hope filled her lungs, then slowly exhaled. The casting director's voice resounded from his seat a few rows back from the stage. "Thank you. All right, next. Hope Bright."

She smoothed her skirt. "Okay. Five, four, three, two, one." Counting backwards was supposed to calm her nerves. It didn't. She threw her shoulders back and strode onto the stage.

Just who was out there past those lights? Hope took a gander at the auditioners as she crossed to the center of the hardwood floor.

The man who appeared to be the director conferred in animated whispers with a woman in an expensive suit. A producer, no doubt. She should wait for their cue.

Hope set her coat down, then took one last glance at the scene in her hands. She ran her fingers through her hair. Finally, the auditioners turned their attention to the stage. "Hi, I'm Hope Bright."

The director nodded for her to start.

"Oh." There would be no chitchat, no niceties. Just like her agent had warned, it would be a tough room. She swallowed, fighting a suddenly parched throat. It was like the Sahara in there. She cleared her windpipe and launched into the reading.

"So, that's how it is. Okay. You know, I told myself a hundred years ago, I was over one-sided relationships and here I am, a fortune in therapy bills later, trying to beg, cajole, plead, whatever it takes to get you to participate in this—"

A pronounced *doink* sounded from her coat pocket. It couldn't be, but it was.

A text had just landed.

Mortified, Hope's jaw slacked. How could she have forgotten to silence the thing? It was a rookie mistake. Rank amateur. All she could do was grab her coat, wrestle the phone out of her pocket and power the thing off so it couldn't embarrass her again. The phone's cheesy shutdown ditty didn't exactly help.

As much as Hope longed to apologize, her training told her otherwise. Simply pick the scene back up, same place, and continue. Stay completely in character:

"—Like I said...I'm trying to do whatever it takes to get you to participate in this... I don't even know what to call what we're doing here. Do you? I mean, I can hardly force a collective pronoun to describe us or it or...will you please just stop staring at me and say something?"

As she finished, Hope propped up her flagging spirit. She braved a look at the director, searching his expression for some semblance of understanding. Even pity. Verbal or nonverbal, any hint of encouragement would do.

None came.

There were no words privately exchanged with the designer-clad producer about her. The director simply jotted a quick note, then excused her with the identically toned "thank you" that he'd used to release the actress just before her. Oh, how she'd come to dread those *thank yous*. They weren't signs of appreciation. They were a saccharine heave-ho. They meant *please leave*. Her insides crushing like a paper cup, Hope willed a smile, then hurried off the stage.

Back inside Hope's apartment, Leanne offered to fix some drinks, then shuffled toward the kitchen. Ivan could at least make himself useful by chatting up Charity and Daniel in the living room. This was way beyond belief. How would she get Frank to believe why she was late if she couldn't half believe it herself?

She pulled a two-liter bottle out of the fridge and sized up the situation. Charity and Daniel had arrived with small suitcases. That sure didn't look good. These two intended to stay. If the girl was family, as she claimed to be, Hope would hardly turn her niece away from her one spare room, the same room Hope had promised to her till the baby came.

Leanne poured the drinks and carried them into the living room. It couldn't hurt to make a good impression. Maybe she could guilt them into staying somewhere else. She handed one glass to Charity and the other to Daniel. "I hope you like Ginger Ale. It's not real ale, you know. Totally non-alcoholic. Even I can have it." She glanced at Hope's wall clock. Ivan wasn't doing squat to carry the conversation. "We have Root Beer, too. That's not actually beer, either. Am I still talking?"

Daniel shook his head. "You're fine.

"Thank you for this," Charity added.

Leanne froze. "Oops. Ivan, are you thirsty?"

Ivan waved her off congenially. "No, thanks." Leanne eased herself down into a seat beside Ivan, across from Charity and Daniel. She caught herself rocking. Why was she rocking? The chair wasn't a rocker. How ridiculous was that? She told herself to sit still, but her toes kept bobbing. That she couldn't seem to stop—even when she slept—at least that's what her mom always told her. A random thought popped into her head. "Hold on. Do you even drink soda?"

"Some do. Some friends of ours even make it. I just haven't had much." Charity raised her glass to her lips and took a tentative drink. Her eyes widened. "Oh. Good."

Leanne rose. "I can get something else."

Daniel held his tumbler, but he didn't take the first sip from it. "This is fine. Really."

Leanne settled back down. Lost for what to do, she wracked her brain for something to say, some bit of jibber-jabber to break up the stupefying silence. Hope's cat, Smokey, wandered out, waltzing into Leanne's line of sight. An inspiration struck. "Are you allergic to cats? Because you probably shouldn't stay here if—"

Charity reached down and stroked Smokey. "Not at all. I like them."

Wouldn't you know it? The cat took to Charity right off the bat. She rubbed herself against those thick black tights Charity was wearing. Leanne couldn't help being disappointed. This was bad.

Daniel set his soda down on a coaster. "Didn't we catch you on your way out, Leanne? Was there somewhere you needed to go?"

Leanne forced a laugh. "Just lollygagging for two, you know?" She fired an irked glance at Ivan.

Charity set her glass down, too. "So. Are you busy getting ready to be parents?"

Ivan shook his head. "Parents? No, no—"

"What?" A spray of spit shot out of Leanne's mouth. She wiped it off Ivan's shoulder. "We're not...married or... I don't actually have a, you know, husband."

Charity looked embarrassed. "Oh, I'm sorry. I shouldn't have—"

Leanne crossed her arms over her middle. Heat rose up her neck, all the way to her ears. "That's such a strange word, coming out of my mouth: *husband*. I mean, I'm barely seventeen, hardly old enough to, you know..." Oh, sweet slobbering succotash! She was only digging herself into a deeper pit. "Anyway...Ivan is, or I should say he was Hope's boyfriend."

Ivan looked at Leanne. "Wait a minute. Stop. What exactly did Hope say to you about us?"

Leanne reared back defensively. "Look-it. Okay, I can't be held responsible for anything I say in my condition. So just...erase, erase, erase!"

Emerging from the theater, Hope yanked the offending cell phone from her pocket and hit the power button. Probably, the text alert had been from her agent, reminding her to let him know how things had gone.

That would be ironic.

81

It also could have been Frank. He was a sport about letting her off for auditions, but the shelf life on his patience usually ran out after an hour or so. Then again, the culprit could have been Ivan. She'd figured she hadn't heard the last of him, and actually, a microscopic part of her wished that were true.

As it turned out, it hadn't been her agent or Ivan. Not even Frank, bugging her to get back to work. Instead, the message was from Leanne:

Hey Hope, S.O.S.!! No ambulance needed, but get your hind parts home pronto! Emergency!!!

What Leanne's version of an emergency was, Hope didn't know, but the number of exclamation points Leanne used set her teeth sideways. She didn't know Leanne well enough to gauge how dire all that punctuation meant the situation actually was. Maybe they'd run out of toilet paper, or the sink had stopped up again. Maybe the apartment building was half on fire.

She punched in her landline at home. Of course, that was when her battery decided to croak. She kicked herself. Why hadn't she remembered to recharge the thing?

Hope dashed through pedestrian traffic, across the blocks to her apartment. She ran just as fast as those cute but not-so-sensible shoes she'd worn to her audition would carry her. They really were starting to rub.

The fact that Leanne didn't want an ambulance was no comfort, not given her financial condition. Still, she was barely even eight months. It was too soon for this to be about the baby. *Or was it?* Who knew if Leanne had calculated her due date right? As far as Hope knew, the closest Leanne had come to prenatal care was one visit to the free clinic. Even then, the line had been so horrendously long, she'd had to bail and get back to work.

Hope's heart beat even faster. The more she gulped for air, the drier her throat became. This could be awful. Disturbing memories flooded back.

No. Please God, no.

Not again.

six

Hope dug deep. Sprinting up three flights of stairs after running from the theater wasn't exactly on her exercise program. A cramp yanked from under her ribs. She winced through the pain. Rounding the last corner, she spotted her door ajar. What in the world? "Leanne?" Hope flung the door open. It clattered against the doorstop.

Leanne popped out of her seat, giddy relief on her face. "Hope! You're here."

Gasping, Hope scanned the room. She did a double take, disbelieving her eyes. She didn't recognize the young Amish man who rose from the sofa, but as soon as the young woman turned, she knew immediately. "Wait, you're... I..." Suddenly lightheaded, Hope steadied herself on Leanne's shoulder. Delight tickled its way across her lips. "*They're* the emergency?"

Leanne shrugged. "Well, yeah, I—"

Before Leanne could finish responding, Hope approached Charity. "You... You're Charity. You don't even have to tell me. I know it." Hope stepped closer as Charity rose. "Come on, up. Let me look at you. Ah, Charity!"

Hope threw her arms around Charity. Why was Ivan there? She would deal with him later. Charity's frame felt so light, yet so strong at the same time. Was she being too familiar too soon? The intensity of the embrace Charity returned gave her all the reassurance she needed.

"How did you know who I was?"

Hope pulled back to arms' length, taking in the details of Charity's features. "How could I not? You look even more like your mamm than you did when you were little."

"That's what Opa says."

"No wonder. I know you're all about being Plain, Charity, but I can't help it. You're so lovely. Just like she was."

Charity brushed Daniel's arm. "Aunt Hope, this is Daniel. Daniel Yoder. You probably knew his father, Mose.

"Yes! And didn't he marry Rachel Schwartz?"

"He did." Daniel looked toward Charity, clearly pleased.

Light danced across Charity's eyes. "Dat asked Daniel to come with me to visit you."

Hope extended a hand to Daniel, regarding him thoughtfully. "Well, then. My brother must trust you very much."

"I'll do my best to live up to that." Daniel shook her hand. His grasp was firm and warm in hers.

For a moment, there was silence. Charity bit at her lips. Hope ping-ponged between the two of them. Just who was Daniel to Charity? Color rose to Charity's cheeks. She fiddled with her sleeve, her eyes communicating what she didn't speak.

Hope nodded softly at Charity, and then gazed back at Daniel. "Yes, Daniel. I'm sure you will."

"We'll be here in the city for three weeks, till Christmas Eve," Daniel said. "We've arranged for rooms at a hostel not far from here."

Hope shook her head. "No, no, please. It's a fleabag. We can cancel. I want you to stay with me."

Charity beamed. "Really? I confess I was kind of hoping you'd ask."

"Good. Then it's settled."

As they chattered on, Hope couldn't help but notice Leanne's face fall. Hope shot an encouraging grin toward her, but it didn't seem to help. The girl just tucked her arms around her bulging abdomen and trudged away. Yes, Hope was over the moon to see Charity, but there was a part of her that ached for Leanne. She knew well what it felt like to be seventeen, the odd one out, completely alone in the world.

Hope drew her coat around herself as she led Ivan outside of her building. All the ease they'd felt together over the passing months was gone. Sure, she'd thought of little else since she'd broken things off with him, but what more could she say? With Charity and Daniel upstairs, she was on overload. She needed her space, and he would just have to understand.

Ivan turned back to Hope. "Daniel could stay at my flat."

Hope sighed. "Ivan, no. I don't think that's a good idea. Besides, your place is tiny."

"And yours is not?"

Once again, a text alert landed. Hope checked it. "It's Frank. I've gotta get back to work."

"Okay."

Hope shivered. "Look, I just don't... Maybe we should detach, you know, not—"

Ivan's face fell. "I thought you liked me. Maybe even loved me."

Hurting Ivan was like kicking a puppy. How could she not do something to soften the blow? She brushed his arm. "I do like you. A lot. I'm just not so much on the marriage track, and you are, so—"

"What is so wrong with getting married?"

"Nothing, Ivan, but ask yourself. Why are you pushing this so soon?"

Ivan took Hope's hand. "We could make a home. Start a family."

Decidedly, Hope let go. She wrestled for words. There was no way to sugarcoat it. "Okay, when does your green card expire?"

"That is not it."

Hope locked eyes with him, standing her ground. "When?"

Breaking her gaze, Ivan exhaled wearily. "I do not exactly know."

"Liar!"

"All right, Hope. Sometime late in January. But I promise you, that is not why I—"

"Of course, it is, Ivan. I get it. You come from an oppressive country. You don't want to have to go back, even though everyone you're connected to is there. So, now you're desperate for an anchor here, someone to secure your place in the free world. It's just...I can't be that person."

"Believe me," Ivan insisted. "It really is not that way. You do not understand."

After so many years of being shunned, it took everything Hope had not to completely recoil. She did her best to stuff it inside. "Trust me, Ivan," she assured. "I understand more than you think."

It was kind of mind-boggling for Hope to imagine that Charity and Daniel would want to go back to work with her, what with all there was to see in New York City. Still, it pleased her that they just wanted to be with her, wherever she needed to go. When she led them into the Café Troubadour, she found Frank at the register, struggling to keep up with the rush.

"Finally. Is that what you call an hour off? Myrna, call Leanne. Get her in here," Frank barked.

As Myrna rang Leanne's cell, Hope fumbled for an excuse. "She said she's not feeling so hot."

"Well, I'm not feeling so hot about being down to four clean plates."

Myrna hung up and grabbed her orders, "She's not picking up."

The agitation in Frank's voice grew. "Call information. Call that employment agency down the street. Hire a temp. Call somebody to get me clean dishes!"

Myrna buttonholed Hope as she approached. "Girl, am I glad to see you back." Myrna passed by Hope, spotting Charity and Daniel just beyond her. "Table for two?"

Hope intervened. "They're with me. Myrna, this is my niece, Charity."

Charity smiled sweetly at Myrna. "Hello, Myrna. So nice to meet you."

Hope's heart filled. "Wow. My niece. It feels so great to say that. And this is Daniel, her—"

With a nod, Daniel rescued her. "I'm Charity's friend from home. Nice to meet you."

Myrna checked toward the kitchen momentarily. "Daniel, you and Charity can make yourselves comfy at whatever table you like, but fair warning, Hope. Dishwasher's fried, Leanne's vapor, and Frank's having himself some kinda holiday hissy fit."

Charity exchanged a glance with Daniel. "I can help."

"Sure, we can," Daniel added.

Hope put a reassuring arm around Charity. "Relax. Honeypot, you just got here."

Charity congenially headed toward the kitchen. "Yes, and it sounds like we're just in time."

Back in the Café's kitchen, Hope prepared a salad. Charity stood at the sink scrubbing. Daniel dried each cleaned plate as Charity rinsed and passed it to him.

Frank fiddled with the disabled automatic dishwasher. Hope nudged him toward Charity and Daniel. Finally, he relented. "Are you sure I can't pay you two something for this?"

Hope stifled a grin. "Better take him up on it. He won't offer twice."

"I already offered twice," Frank blustered. "This is twice."

Charity turned back to Frank. "It's fine. Really. We're happy to help."

Frank scowled in frustration at the dishwasher. "Blasted piece of high-tech junk! Thing crashes every time you blink." He looked up at Daniel as Hope headed out with the salad. "You wouldn't know anything about—"

Daniel shrugged apologetically.

Frank slapped his own forehead. "What in blazes am I talking about? You people have the right idea. You work with your own hands. Hands, you can depend on. Hands don't blow a fuse. Hands don't crash."

Hope couldn't help her amusement as she passed through the swinging kitchen doors. She smoothly served the salad to Goldie where he sat on a stool at the counter. He'd been her customer so long; she knew exactly what he liked. He preened over her attention, so attend to him, she did. "Half Cobb, chopped. Hold the egg yolk, crispy bacon— turkey, not pork. Light balsamic on the side."

Goldie motioned back toward the kitchen, a sardonic sneer on his face. "So, what? Did the Mayflower just dock?"

Well accustomed, Hope took Goldie's caustic humor in stride. "They're not time-travelers, Goldie. They're Amish."

Goldie drizzled dressing on his salad. "Very quaint, but what are they doing back in the kitchen?"

Hope stuck her hand out to receive his empty dressing cup. "The dishes you're eating off, at the moment."

Goldie eyed Charity and Daniel uneasily through the pass-through window. "I don't know about you, but religious people give me the willies." He stuffed a first bite into his mouth.

Hope tipped her head. "Really?"

A spot of dressing glistened on Goldie's chin. "Pretend to be all sweet and pure, but I watch those exposés on TV. I know better. Those people have got huge issues."

Unintimidated, Hope answered. "They're my family. She is, at least."

Goldie's jaw dropped. "Oh. What...you mean, you're—"

With a perky smile, Hope headed back toward the kitchen. "Congratulations, Goldie. You've outed me. Yes. I'm Amish."

Never had Hope been so glad to be back at her apartment. With Charity and Daniel there, it felt full in ways it never had before, and not just when it came to improvising accommodations.

Hope spread one of her handmade quilts over the sofa for Daniel. She'd never tired of looking at that particular quilt. The piecework formed an expansive tree. Laden with colorful autumn leaves, its boughs reached out against cornflower blue heavens with white clouds.

Embroidered on many of the leaves were the names of her Amish ancestors. All the dates were there, too. It chronicled the years anyone had been born or married into the Bright family, extending from the eighteenth century, all the way up to the births of Charity's twin brothers Aaron and Isaac. How she longed to see those two boys.

Her heart warmed as Charity and Daniel leaned in to examine her work. It had been time-consuming, but knowing how that quilt would make them feel made every hour spent on it worthwhile. Charity would recognize the quality of the stitching. It was fine, just as her mother had taught her. It told of many more nights engrossed in this solitary pastime than she cared to admit to most people. Hopefully, they'd see that it also spoke of the bond she felt with those she'd left behind. They were all still part of her. They always would be.

Daniel traced the family line, all the way up the branches until he located Charity's name. It was stitched on a vibrant yellow leaf. "There you are, Charity."

Charity studied the quilt, transfixed. "This is so beautiful, Aunt Hope. Ah, there's Oma and Opa. See, Daniel? Faith and Eli Bright."

"It's the whole Bright family tree, as much as I know, all the way from when they left Switzerland. You know, I'd always wondered why we call our grandparents *Oma* and *Opa* instead of *Dawdi* and *Mammi* like so many there do. It goes back to our Swiss-German roots."

Charity marveled. "So, our family—we're from Switzerland?"

"Yep...where the whole Amish faith began." Aunt Hope gestured to the top of the quilt. "See, in the sky? Those are pieces cut from my old dresses. The clouds, they came from my Sunday apron."

Daniel traced through the generations. "How did you find out about all of this family history?"

Hope grimaced. "Would it taint it for you if I told you I got a lot of it off the Internet? You know about the Internet, right?"

Daniel nodded acceptingly. "These people from the seventeen hundreds—so, they spelled the surname B-r-e-c-h-t. When did they change the spelling to B-r-i-g-h-t?"

"Right there." Hope pointed to the first of the Bright leaves. "See, Simon and Anna Bright. The dates track with when the family immigrated to this country. Since Brecht is pronounced the same way as Bright, I guess with the language barrier it was heard and recorded as Bright when they registered here. Now, there are Brights all over Pennsylvania."

"And at least one New York City," Charity smiled.

"Yeah. At least one." Hope released a bittersweet sigh. What a joy it was to see Charity now, but all the growing up years she had missed— they were forever gone.

Hope looked around her apartment. In all of the time she'd lived there, it had never felt so much like home as it did at that very moment, even with the makeshift arrangements. It confirmed what she had always believed, that home wasn't so much a particular dwelling place as it was just being with those that she loved. After seventeen years away from family, that sense of home was nothing less than a healing balm.

Charity covered a yawn. It had been a long day for everyone and morning would come quickly. Charity traded goodnights with Daniel, then headed into Hope's room to get ready for bed.

Daniel stuffed a feather pillow into a cotton case. "Thank you for making room for us."

Hope set the sofa's back cushions aside. "You sure this will be okay? Under the circumstances I could always ask..." Hope cocked her head toward Leanne as the girl eased herself onto the futon in the spare room.

Daniel leaned in so as not to be overheard. "Charity will be with you. Leanne will have her place. I'll be fine out here."

There was a kindness and maturity about Daniel that Hope couldn't help but appreciate. He reminded her of the gentler folk of her Amish upbringing. So often they put the needs of others far ahead of themselves. Already, she liked him. "Okay, then. *Guten nacht*, Daniel."

Daniel smiled as he pulled back the blanket. "*Guten nacht.*"

Hope started to leave, then returned to him. A thought nagged her mind. "I hope I didn't... I mean, when first I introduced you at the café, I didn't know exactly what to call you, how exactly you and Charity...you know."

Daniel returned an understanding smile. "We should wait to let Charity speak for herself. But between us, I have your brother's blessing to call her my Special Friend."

Hope nodded. "No small feat, knowing Nathan.

"He's a good man, her Dat."

"Yes." Hope headed back toward her room. "So he is."

Standing in her bathroom with Charity, Hope could still hardly believe it. The inquisitive three year-old child she'd left behind was gone. There, splashing her face with water at her side, was a mature young woman.

Though she did her best to suppress it, regret knotted in Hope's throat. *Oh, to turn back the clock.* Aunts should be close with their nieces. Why couldn't she scurry back across the years? If she could she would gather up every frayed end between them and tie them all neatly together. She expelled a resigned breath. Those were bonds that could only be forged over time.

How naturally beautiful Charity was, her dark lashes accenting crystal blue eyes. In contrast, Hope rubbed on cold cream to remove her waterproof mascara. "I used to do that."

Charity pressed a towel to her face. "Do what?"

"Just wash my face. Soap and water. That was before the days of volumized lashes and flawless finish foundation."

Charity hung up her towel. "You don't like makeup?"

Hope chuckled. That was so far from the case. "I like makeup too much, actually. Addicted in a way. To that and my smart phone. You watch. I will never set foot out of my apartment without either one."

Charity turned to face her. "I don't know much about phones, but I like how you look as you are."

Hope knew it wasn't like the Amish to flatter. Still, she didn't entirely believe it. "There's Plain and there's plain." She wandered back into her adjacent bedroom, tossing her smudged tissue into the trash.

Charity followed. "You sound like Bethany. My best friend. At home."

Hope turned down the quilt on her queen-sized bed. On this one, she'd stitched Double Wedding Rings in soft lavender, rose, and moss green calicos, framed by candlelight muslin. She wondered if Charity would think it an odd choice of pattern for a single woman's bed. "So, how are things? At home." It was both strange and wonderful to call Amish Country home again, after all this time.

Affection crossed Charity's face as she rounded the bed to the other side. "Dat never changes."

"Never did, never will."

Charity drew back the quilt on her side. "This is so pretty. Is it one of yours, too?"

"It is," Hope replied. "I saved it for years, but... Well, I guess I never..." Weddings that had never materialized drifted through Hope's mind. Jonathan had long since married, cheated, and been divorced by someone else. Leo was... Something soured in her stomach. It felt like protection that things hadn't worked out so well with Leo. James had been

SUSAN ROHRER

another story. James, she had loved. She'd spent years getting over him. Then, there was Ivan. *What to do about Ivan...* Hope turned down her side of the quilt. "Anyway, maybe one day."

Charity crawled into bed. "You should see Aaron and Isaac. They're taller than I am."

Hope tried to imagine it. Unless the boys strongly favored their parents, she knew she'd never recognize them now. "Out here, we'd show pictures. Photos."

"I've seen a lot of photographs in town," Charity said. "But they're flat...and so still, doncha know?"

Hope considered it thoughtfully.

"All the pictures I have in my mind, they're alive," Charity added. "They move. I like that."

Hope nodded, remembering. "Yeah. I did, too." Her mind wandered back to those she missed so much. "And my father? How is he?"

"Opa? He's well. He lives with us, now, since... Did you know that Oma passed?"

Something caught in Hope's throat. She could only bring herself to nod. Leaving her mother had been the most excruciating parting of all. Years ago, to hear of her death had been nothing less than shattering.

A familiar pang cut through her. In very real ways, she was still mourning. Old questions

100

resurfaced. Had she made the right decision not to try and attend that service? Should she have come to English world at all? She could hardly bring herself to look at Charity. "It was the one time your father wrote to me. Short. And it was all in Pennsylvania German, of course, but... What can I say?"

Charity situated her pillow. "Seven summers ago, now. I really miss her."

How soothing. Finally, there was someone there who shared a sense of her grief. "I've missed her, too, Charity. More than I can say."

Charity turned. "Aunt Hope, I'm sorry. If it's too painful—"

Hope brushed Charity's shoulder fondly. "No, Sweetie. It's a good hurt."

Hope relaxed onto her side of the bed. "I have these pictures in my mind, too. She was—present company excepted—she was the very hardest to leave."

A moment of silence passed between them. Did she dare ask? Hope gathered her courage. "My mother...did she ever speak of me?"

The empathy that came over Charity's face was telling.

"You don't have to answer that, Charity. I shouldn't have asked you." Still, she could see the regret lingering in Charity's eyes. "It's okay. Mamm, your Oma...she was so good. So devout. Of course, she wouldn't have said anything. She couldn't even say my name."

"It was Dat who told me about you," Charity whispered. "Just days ago, because I found your Christmas card. By accident. He hadn't opened it."

"He never does."

"I didn't either. We just used the address to find your place. I was surprised, really. It's not like Dat to leave things in his pockets on washday. He knows I empty them before I do the clothes."

"No. It's not like him. At least it wasn't years ago." Hope mulled it over, knowing her brother. Did this represent a softening of his resolve? "And who was it that decided you could come?"

Charity snugged the quilt around her neck. "Dat. On two conditions: that I'd come with Daniel, and that I'd be home before Christmas."

Hope knew her brother, well enough to guess that there was more than Charity's visit at play. Like Noah in the ark, Nathan had sent a gentle dove out to test the waters. He was, no doubt, praying for her return. He was also hoping to gain Daniel as a son-in-law in the bargain.

"Is it true what Dat says?" Charity asked. "Am I really like my mamm so much? I mean beyond the physical resemblance."

There were few people Hope thought of more highly than Charity's mother, Grace. A fond smile came to her lips. "Your mamm..." *Where to begin?* "Well, everyone needs a Bethany. And your mamm, she was mine. Always full of surprises and still somehow so...grounded. You know?"

"*Ja.* Dat always said she was steady as an oak in a windstorm."

"That she was."

"He planted one in our yard the year she passed. It's grown tall, now."

Hope studied Charity's face. "It's not that you look exactly like she did. There is a very strong resemblance, though. You remind me a bit of Nathan, too. But mostly, it's Grace's light there in your eyes. Even when you were a little thing I could see that."

"We still set a place for her at Christmas every year."

The thought touched Hope. "Really?"

Charity propped herself up on her elbow. "We make her best dishes, sing her favorite hymns. Oma taught me all of their recipes before she died. So, we set a place, and we talk about how much we miss her, and how blessed we were to have her. At least I do. Dat most of all. Aaron and Isaac never knew her, so they...well, they're seventeen, and—"

Hope understood. "Not so much on Memory Lane?"

Charity looked puzzled. "Memory Lane?"

"Just an English expression," Hope explained. "It's like you go walking down those old paths and, just in your head, you go there."

"Oh," Charity replied. "Do you go there?"

Hope savored the question. How rare it was to have someone to ask about such things. "I do go there, Charity. All the time. It's part of my work."

"At the Café Troubadour?"

"That's where it started, at the café. It's where my agent first heard me sing." Hope hesitated. Performing wasn't something the Amish did, but it was part of who she'd become. "So, then he signed me, started sending me out for stuff. I booked here and there—jingles, voice-overs, small plays once in a while. It's strange. I never trained. It started out as kind of a lark, really. Next thing I knew, it was a full-blown passion. Now, waiting tables, that's just the work I do so I can survive. The paying the bills part. But when I'm on stage, where I'm working on getting more work, that's when I really live."

Charity's eyes widened. "You get up in front of people on stage here?"

"It's a long way from back on the farm, but yeah," Hope admitted. "Maybe there's something pathological about it—I'm sure there is—but...I do. This therapist said I sort of have this need to, I don't know...to be seen or acknowledged. She said it all goes back to the shunning. Maybe she's right."

Hope pondered it for a moment. "When I'm there on stage, that's when I go down Memory Lane. Underneath whatever or wherever it is, I'm saying, there's this other life there. My life back there with all of you. So, the stage...that's one place where I'm completely free. I can go back home."

For a little while, they rested there silently. Her words hung in the air.

"Do you ever think about giving that up, about really coming back?" Charity asked.

"All the time, Charity. All the time." Hope reached over and flicked off the lamp. As early as they would need to rise, it was past time to call it a night. Still, long after Charity closed her eyes in slumber, Hope lay awake. Her mind simply refused to rest.

She had not left the fold in rebellion. That she knew. There was no family tension that had driven her away. It was nothing like that at all. It was her sense of principle that had separated them. That principle could come to part them again in just a few weeks' time. If she refused to compromise, once more, it would leave her in the bitter throes of grief. It would tear at her soul, leaving her ravaged all over again.

seven

Though the sun had yet to peek over the horizon, Charity busied herself preparing a hot breakfast. Daniel was awake, too. He'd already folded up his linens and put all the cushions back in place on the couch. The aroma of hotcakes and scrambled eggs would gently coax the others out of their warm beds.

Indeed, it wasn't very long before Hope and Leanne joined them around the table she'd set. As soon as they were all seated, Daniel wordlessly bowed his head. Noticing him, Leanne bugged her eyes awkwardly, but Hope gave her an encouraging nod, and then bowed her head as well.

Charity hid her amusement. She closed her eyes and silently said the Lord's Prayer, just as she knew Daniel would. How thankful she felt to be there with him at her Aunt Hope's table. Soon, she heard Daniel, and then Aunt Hope, let out a breath. There. They were finished, too.

Charity raised her eyes and smiled softly at Daniel. It was gratifying to see him lead the way in blessing what she'd prepared.

Leanne glanced around the table, a baffled look on her face. "What? Is that it?"

Aunt Hope reached for the bowl of eggs. "That's it." She passed the eggs to Leanne. "Doesn't this look great? I'm trying to remember the last time I actually ate a hot breakfast."

Charity unfolded her napkin and set it on her lap. "Dat always said he thought it was the best meal of the day."

Leanne passed the eggs to Daniel with a queasy expression. "Yeah, well something tells me your Dat never had a case of morning sickness."

Charity blushed. Talk of pregnancy in mixed company would take a bit of getting used to yet, especially in front of Daniel. She handed a platter of hotcakes to Leanne. "I've heard that starting with a dry bread like this can help with that, to settle your stomach."

Hope took a sip of hot coffee. "And when you have to be at work by sunrise...speaking of which, Leanne, I take it you're going in?"

Leanne pouted. "Didn't get up in the dark for nothin'."

Hope set her mug down. "Hate to break it to you, but the dishwasher's fried."

Leanne slumped. "Not again. You know I can't hardly keep up by hand."

Charity passed the hash browns to Leanne. "We'll come help."

"Sure, we will," Daniel echoed.

"No thanks," Leanne groused, handing off the potatoes to Hope. "Like I need to lose the only job I ever had on account of you two showin' me up." Abruptly, Leanne rose from the table.

Hope quickly caught Leanne's arm. "Leanne, they didn't mean—"

Shaking free, Leanne quickly left the kitchen. "I gotta go."

Charity flushed. She had only meant well, but obviously she'd upset Leanne. She watched, mortified, as Leanne grabbed her coat and left the apartment. Charity turned to Aunt Hope as she began to rise. "I'm so sorry. Should I try to—"

Hope reached out and took her hand. That alone was comforting. "You did nothing wrong, Charity. Don't apologize. Just sit. She's kind of hormonal, and more than a little bit threatened. Confused. Ferhuddled, as the Amish would say. Try not to worry. It'll pass."

Charity eased back into her chair. Surely, Aunt Hope was right. People were the way they were for reasons. Yes, Leanne had her reasons, her private fears and pains. She tried to imagine what it would feel like to be in Leanne's predicament...pregnant and alone in the big city, with no family, and no place to call home. No wonder the girl was on edge.

"I just wish I could afford to take the day off to spend with you two," Hope said, "but I'm barely making rent, much less groceries."

Daniel downed his hotcakes hungrily. "Maybe I could pick up some work while we're here. Help out."

"Nothing doing," Hope answered. "This is your Rumspringa. It's supposed to be fun. Run around. Check out the sights. See what the world is like."

Daniel knit his brow pleasantly. "Looks like to me that people have to work in the world. I wouldn't feel right not earning my keep."

Charity smiled. How much Daniel reminded her of her father—so hard working, even at a time like this. There was much to be admired about Daniel's character. That was for certain. But as he talked with Aunt Hope, she also couldn't help but take in his other qualities. Those warm brown eyes of his were so engaging. There was also his strong, clean-shaven jaw, and the pleasant tone of his voice. How had she resisted him so long?

Hope guzzled the rest of her orange juice and rose from the table. "Well...wish I could say I don't need help, but the truth is, it wouldn't hurt about now. Although..." She grabbed a dog-eared booklet off her shelf and handed it to Daniel. "If you really want to help out while you're here, you might want to look this over."

Daniel read the booklet's cover. "G.E.D. study guide?"

"Ivan left it. It's a test, to get your high school equivalency." Hope rose from the table. "Ivan needed his so he could get into cooking school. He's just been shining shoes to pay his way through. Not that he'll be able to finish here now, but the equivalency really opened up his options. First thing I did when I got here was to go for my G.E.D. No way to get decent paying work without it."

Hope reached to clear her dishes, but Charity put out a hand. "I'll take care of that."

Daniel set the G.E.D. booklet aside. "I'm an experienced carpenter. I'll find something."

As Hope left the kitchen, Charity exchanged an understanding glance with Daniel. She examined the G.E.D booklet.

Hope called out from her room. "I totally get it that you don't need an equivalency back at home. And it's silly because you sound like you're probably smarter than most of the high school graduates out here. Crazy, I know, but having that piece of paper does make a difference when you apply."

Charity monitored Daniel's reaction. Why had this topic even come up? Sure, the English favored much more formal education than Amish youth were required to complete. But would Daniel feel any less worthy of respect than he was, just because he didn't have their stamp of approval?

Daniel leaned toward Charity, lowering his voice. "She seems to think we're staying longer than we are."

Charity put the booklet down. "Last night, you told her we'd leave in three weeks. Christmas Eve. Maybe it's just about paying the bills till then."

Daniel referred to the booklet. "But this...I've heard about it. It's far beyond eighth grade material. I'd have to study on it a good while. By the time I'd be ready to take the test, it'd be time to leave."

"Don't worry with it, Daniel. You've already learned so much in your carpentry trade. This isn't about that."

"*Ja*, well..." Daniel downed the last of his eggs.

"I guess it's natural that she'd want us to stay. Of course she does. Just like we want her to come home. But maybe if we try to be open to her suggestions, later on she'll be open to ours."

The sound of approaching footsteps quieted her. Aunt Hope was returning.

Aunt Hope leaned over to kiss her cheek. "Come by for lunch, okay? It'll be on me."

Charity searched her aunt's face. "Are you sure Leanne will be comfortable with us being there?"

"She'll have to be," Hope assured "We're family."

Strolling along with Daniel, Charity scanned the streets of Manhattan. Holiday decorations sparkled in the sunlight, reminding shoppers that Christmas was coming.

A Salvation Army bell ringer stood by a shiny red bucket with a slit in the top. Just like the ones Charity had seen in town, the man rang his little bell continuously, soliciting for contributions. Electric signs flashed. Horns blared. In contrast to the placid, rolling hills of home, the downtown sights and sounds were still a little overwhelming. It made her thankful to have Daniel there at her side.

Suddenly, he took her hand.

It was almost as if he'd sensed how oddly disconnected she felt. Maybe he'd been feeling the same way. She drank in the sensation of his grasp for the very first time. His hand was so reassuring, so comfortable in hers.

At home, he would never have been so bold, at least not in public. But far from home and the watchful eyes of those who lived there, Daniel Yoder was holding her hand. In that place where she felt so very different from everyone else, it gave her a sense of belonging.

Pedestrian traffic there certainly had a brisk flow, like in town when they went to market, only much more so. Deliberately, Charity matched Daniel's leisurely pace. He was not afraid to be different. A lesser man might try to either blend or keep up, but not Daniel.

A wide variety of people populated this city, all the way from smartly dressed business types to the wandering homeless, to the darkly foreboding, to those she could only describe as fashionably unique. There was hair in shocking candy colors on a few. Tattoos were everywhere. Despite the diversity, with her bonnet and cape, and Daniel's Amish hat, there was no escaping how much they stood out in the crowd. They were in this world, but nothing at all felt like they were anywhere near of it.

Almost out of nowhere, a street vendor stepped in front of Daniel. He thrust a gleaming woman's watch into Daniel's free hand. "Got some sweet designer time-pieces here. This one here would look mighty fine on your woman's wrist this Christmas."

"No, thank you." Daniel extended the watch back toward the vendor. "We don't wear—"

All at once, Charity heard a familiar sound: the clip-clopping of hooves on pavement. "Oh. Look, Daniel. A horse."

The vendor whipped around. A mounted police officer was approaching. "Time to beat the heat, if you know what I mean." In a flash, the vendor wrapped up his wares and bolted, leaving Daniel standing there with the watch.

Daniel called after him. "Wait! Your watch."

Ignoring him, the vendor quickly dashed into the crowd and disappeared around the nearest corner.

Charity traded a perplexed look with Daniel. She gestured toward the watch. "What should we do with that?"

Just then, a harried businessman barged through, banging right into her. In the jolt, he sloshed steaming coffee on his pants, but most of it splashed on her. Charity felt the heat of it soak through her skirt, but the man seemed only worried about himself.

"Great!" the man griped. He swiped a hand across his trousers. "That's just perfect." Angrily, he tossed his coffee cup into a trashcan and hustled down the street.

With concern in his eyes, Daniel turned to Charity. "Is that hot?"

Charity stopped on the sidewalk to brush the coffee off her dress. "It's nothing. I'm fine."

A woman groused from behind them. "Hey, move it or lose it!"

Realizing she was blocking the way, Charity stepped aside from the flow of traffic. Daniel quickly followed. He retrieved a handkerchief from his pocket and offered it to Charity.

As she blotted the coffee, Charity glanced up at the passing throng. Few made eye contact with anything but their electronic devices. "So many people. Everyone's in such a hurry. Do you suppose any of them actually like it here?" Something about the absurdity of it all made it almost amusing.

"I don't know." Daniel scratched behind his ear, a little grin forming. There were those dimples of his. He examined the abandoned watch. "Reminds me of my uncle's hives. Everyone buzzing by, pressed in tight, so intent to get to wherever it is they're going."

Charity nodded. "It really is like that, isn't it?" As she straightened, her eyes fell on the paper machine beside them. It advertised free job listings. "Daniel, look. Jobs. Maybe there would be something temporary for you."

Daniel set the watch down on top of the vending machine and pulled out a paper. It was not thirty seconds before a teenager reached in, snatched the timepiece, and sprinted away.

Charity could hardly believe it. Just yesterday, they'd happened upon that job listings paper. Today, there they were, seated in a Manhattan employment office. The agent wasn't the friendliest of fellows, but she was thankful to see how busily he scanned his computer screen for job possibilities, popping his lips all the while. Surely, there must be something in there.

Charity smiled at Daniel. He really wanted to do what he could to help her Aunt Hope in any way he could, even if just for a little while.

The employment agent hacked loudly, a phlegmy cough rattling through his chest. He cleared his throat and glanced at Daniel. "Your aunt was right. Without a G.E.D. you'll get nothing but grunt work."

Daniel referred to the job listing paper. "I noticed there's something for framers here. I have six years of carpentry experience."

The agent peered at them over his reading glasses. "As you might guess, they use power tools here. Did you also notice it's union? Somehow, I'm guessing you're not."

Charity saw Daniel's face fall. She longed to encourage him.

The agent rubbed his right wrist. "Carpal Tunnel is killing me." Again, he hacked. "Look, I get that you've put up a few places out there in the country. But this is the Big Apple. You got any hands-on experience here in the city at anything whatsoever?"

Daniel exchanged a glance with Charity. "We've, uh... Well, we've filled in a little, so we did. Doing dishes at this restaurant in town."

"And I can cook," Charity added.

The agent checked the listings on his computer again. "Pro chefs are lined up all round the block to cook. That's not gonna happen. Okay. Let's see, let's see..."

Charity found herself holding her breath as the agent hunched over his computer, tapping the same button over and over. On and on, he scanned down his computer screen.

Finally, the man looked up. With a tip of his head, he swiveled his screen around for them to see. "Well, ho, ho, ho, and a Merry Christmas! The Café Troubadour just posted for a dishwasher this morning. Might get a jump on that."

Charity blanched. Reading a computer screen for the first time was daunting. There was so much information. Finally, there it was. The job listing. Frank Abernathy's name was right there as the contact. Sure enough, the Café Troubadour was where Aunt Hope worked, and that dishwasher position was Leanne's. Charity glanced at Daniel, disturbed in the pit of her stomach. Frank was already taking steps to find Leanne's replacement.

eight

Hope tucked herself behind the Café Troubadour's counter. Quickly, she pulled out her cell and checked her voice message alerts.

Nothing.

It had not been the first time she'd checked that morning, not to mention the day before that. Every hour, on the hour, she'd stopped. She couldn't help it. Surely, there would have been word about the status of her audition by now. That is, if there was ever to be any word at all. The New York "Slow No" was definitely the worst part of this process.

Why people couldn't call your agent and let you know when you didn't get a callback, she'd never understand. Rejection tasted rotten, but at least there was something good served by it. Getting rejected meant you could start trying to deal with your disappointment. You could pry your fingers off what you'd wanted so much, and begin the process of letting go. This way, for at least a few days—a week if you were especially pathetic—you kept staring at your phone. You kept the itty-bitty fantasy that they might still want you alive. It was the same every last gut-scraping time. Even after you tanked.

Myrna sidled up next to Hope. She started to butter some toast. "No word yet?"

Hope pocketed her cell. "This is crazy-making."

Myrna gave her an understanding squeeze. "Baby, either that director calls you back or it's his loss."

Hope leaned back against the counter. "Maybe it's better this way. With Charity and Daniel here. What, am I going to work here days, rehearse every night, and never even see them?" Hope sighed. "Why am I obsessing over this?"

"Pursuing your dream?" Myrna served Goldie his toast.

"Which one?" Hope asked.

Goldie twisted on his stool at the counter. "Would you like to hear my oh, so very humble opinion?"

Hope cast a half-mast glance at Goldie. "Yes, Goldie. More than anything."

Goldie spread a glaze of orange marmalade on his sourdough bread. "I say you're compensating."

Hope rubbed her neck. Why had she even opened that door?

"You know they don't remember your name, much less your phone number," Goldie gloated, "because they have no intention whatsoever of singling you out from the hordes of marginally talented wannabes, all drooling for their attention."

Hope just shook her head. She would not let on that Goldie was getting to her.

"So, you rationalize that, of course, the timing is all wrong," he prattled. "You should be with your family, who, in some kind of psycho-ironic twist, has banned you just as surely as the Broadway stage has. Only you can't accept that, so you're..." He flipped his wrist over to extend an open palm and the conversational floor to Hope.

"Compensating." Just then, Hope noticed that Charity and Daniel had arrived. A reprieve. Quickly, she excused herself.

Frank put two steaming plates on the kitchen pass-through for Myrna as Hope scooted by sideways. "Order up!"

As discreetly as possible, Hope examined the dishwasher job posting. Charity and Daniel looked on as Leanne bussed a table nearby.

"What should we do?" Charity whispered.

Hope shook her head. "I don't know. Looks like a guillotine or a noose to me."

A look of confusion crossed Daniel's face. "What?"

"No matter what, it's not so great," Hope explained. "If you do take it, she'll think you edged her out and if you don't—"

Daniel nodded, catching on. "Then Frank will just hire someone else."

Charity tucked the job listing away. "Either way, Leanne loses her job. What else can she get in her condition?"

Hope straightened, pointing up with her index finger. "Unless we make a deal."

Hope peeked into the kitchen. As usual Frank was working triple-time. How perfect.

Hope ushered Charity and Daniel through the swinging doors. They waited discreetly by the entry while Hope approached Frank at the griddle. Deliberately, she situated herself so he couldn't miss the growing pile of dirty dishes, pots, and pans just over her shoulder. Frank was a bottom-line kind of boss. When he got desperate enough, he'd allow a bit of wiggle room. As long as it wouldn't cost him anything more than he'd already offered, he might just consider it.

Hope explained how things could work as concisely as she could. The fewer words, the better with Frank. He continued to prep dinner plates all the while. It was hard to tell if he was listening at all.

Finally, he shook his head. "Can't hire but one of them if I keep Leanne."

Hope didn't miss a beat. "Charity will do it. And Daniel can be on standby in case Leanne flakes."

"I dunno," Frank started. "All I got's what I got, even if I'm paying two of them to split it."

"Fine," Hope agreed. "But Sunday's off. Same as me. Just pull in relief crew to cover that."

Frank looked over Daniel's and Charity's Amish garb, a dubious expression forming. "An apron's enough for him, but she's gotta wear a uniform."

Satisfied, Hope shook Frank's hand. "I'll work on it."

Leanne padded into Hope's living room. It was hard enough to figure out how to behave in someone else's house, much less with an Amish dude plopped right there on the sofa. But really. Just because Daniel was sleeping there at night didn't mean he owned the place. It was the living room, for cryin' out loud. The television should be fair game.

Leanne snatched the remote and flipped on the set. "You don't mind, do you?" She eased herself down into an overstuffed chair.

Daniel looked up from perusing a booklet. It said G.E.D. on the cover.

Great. He must be sticking around for a while. Leanne zapped her way through the channels. There was hardly a thing worth more than half a second's time. She turned the set back off. "Nothing on anyway."

He just smiled a little, and then went right back to reading.

Not so chatty, she guessed. "I used to like that show where the rich girl was crushin' on this poor boy and... You probably never watched that show."

Daniel shook his head, his brows raised.

Leanne studied him. "No TV, no radio, no computer, no texting, nothin'?"

"Not really."

"Seriously?" That was just plain wacko. What did a person possibly do without all of those things? "Don't you get bored?"

Daniel turned a page in the booklet. "There's always something to do when you live on a farm."

"I mean like fun. What do you do for fun?"

Daniel put the booklet down and rose from the couch. "Well, there are lots of things. I can show you one." He went to his suitcase and opened it up. "I have a little brother and a younger sister. So, with Christmas coming, I always like to make them something."

Homemade presents? *Really?* Way too much work. "Why don't you just go to the store and buy it?"

A twinkle sparked in Daniel's eye. "Because that wouldn't be as much fun."

From the corner of his suitcase, Daniel pulled out a carving project. He handed over what looked like a miniature wooden buggy in progress. Leanne examined it.

Daniel held up an uncarved block. "There's a horse in this piece. You just can't see it yet."

Leanne looked the carving over skeptically. "And you think he'll actually like that?"

Daniel nodded. "I can understand why you might not. But he will."

Leanne thought of her kid brother, Jay. Video games, computers, and science kits—that's what the Jaybird would like. "My brother always gives me a list a mile long and there hasn't never once been a horse or a buggy on it."

"We could make him one," Daniel suggested.

Leanne sighed. Daniel just didn't get it. He didn't know Jay-Jay, not at all.

A thickness came over her throat. She tried to rub it away. Man, she missed that kid brother of hers. Forget how nerdy he was or what a pain in the patooty he could be. She just wanted to see his pudgy little face.

Her parents floated through her mind. She ached for them most of all. Being away from them sure was a hard lump to swallow, like taking one of those big chalky vitamins that stuck side-to-side on the way down. The poke of being apart just wouldn't leave, no matter how she tried to wash it away. Whatever. There was no way she could let any of that show.

She heaved a sigh and handed the carving back to Daniel. "Thanks, but...don't think I'll be seeing my brother this year."

Charity watched as Aunt Hope rifled through her bedroom closet. Colorful sweaters and print dresses hung across the bar. There were also quite a few pairs of jeans. Actually, except for the white blouse, piping, and buttons, the Troubadour's dark green jumpers were just about the closest thing in there to an Amish dress. They even included a matching white apron.

Aunt Hope pulled one of her uniforms out and held it by the hanger. "You think?"

Charity looked it over. It wasn't as bad as other skirts she'd seen in town, but it was definitely shorter than she was used to wearing.

Give it a chance.

She held the uniform against her body. "Ooh," she cringed. It would hit just above her knee.

Everything in her wanted to help out at the café, but she couldn't help feeling torn. How could she wear this without feeling completely self-conscious? "Oh, Aunt Hope... I don't know."

"I really do remember that feeling, Charity." Her expression had understanding written all over it. "You'll get used to it."

Charity folded the uniform over. "Won't people stare at my legs?"

Aunt Hope lifted the apron's laces. "It's not exactly a fashion statement. Actually, you'll get more stares in what you're wearing right now. And hey. At least it's a solid color."

Charity perched on the bed. "To be honest, it just feels like...like I'd be violating some kind of..." Charity stopped. What they were talking about went far beyond the appropriate length for a woman's skirt. It was about much more. It was about the woman underneath the skirt, and who it was that she'd decided to be at her heart.

Then again, the last thing Charity wanted to do was to make Aunt Hope feel bad about the choices she had made. This was a skirt-length she wore all the time, apparently without a second thought. She searched Aunt Hope's face with concern. "Can you tell me something?"

Aunt Hope sat down beside her. "Sure. Anything."

"You were raised Plain," Charity started, "just like we were."

Aunt Hope nodded. "That's right."

"You left all of us, but was it more than that? Did it mean leaving your faith, too?"

Aunt Hope took Charity's hand in hers. "Oh, Sweetie, no. Not at all. I didn't leave my faith."

It was hard to understand, but still... What a relief it was to hear those words. "You didn't?"

Aunt Hope smiled softly. "Oh, I guess I 'ran around' longer than I should have at first, and it must have seemed to my brother that I'd gone completely off the rails, but then... You know what I found out? See, Charity, I found out that God... He's so much bigger than I used to think. He's all over Amish Country, yeah. But turns out He's all over the place, here in the English world, too."

Charity's mind clouded. "I do know that. They teach us to respect people of other faiths. But being Plain people... The Bible, it talks about coming out from the world, about being separate."

"You know, it might surprise you, Charity, but I still read my Bible most every day."

A weight lifted off Charity. "You do?"

Hope nodded. "The same Bible that talks about being separate also says to be in the world but not of it." Hope opened the worn Bible on her nightstand and flipped through its pages. There were underlines and highlights. Little notes extended into the margins. "Look here, it says 'Go ye into all the world and preach the Gospel.' Jesus' words. Not mine."

Never once had Charity questioned what she'd been taught. But seeing the words of her Lord, there in red amongst the black and white, she could hardly find room to argue.

Hope set her Bible aside. "I don't know. Maybe it's just that different people get different marching orders. Maybe you're called to stay inside and I'm called to stay out. And if I'm in pants or in my uniform or in my footie pajamas that have holes in them, it doesn't matter. I guess I've made peace with that. It's all good."

Still unsure, Charity took it in. "You go to the English churches?"

Hope smiled. "I go to the same one as Myrna. Ivan sings in the choir, too—more of a joyful noise, really. But trust me, Charity. No matter what anybody says, you have not been to church till you've gone at least one time with Myrna."

Charity took a seat in the church pew between Daniel and Aunt Hope. Her breath felt shallow in her chest. The sanctuary alone was a far cry from anything she'd ever seen. For starters, the place was much larger than the home church where they gathered every other week.

Vaulted ceilings with exposed beams reached toward the sky. Colored light shone in through intricate stained glass. The way those windows were pieced together almost reminded her of a quilt. Festive Christmas decorations were all about the sanctuary. Tiny white electric lights twinkled on a tree covered with handmade ornaments, all in white and gold. There were stringed instruments and a piano, an organ, even drums.

Mostly, though, it was the crowd. Charity turned to look behind them.

Hundreds were already there; more streamed down the aisles. Singles, families, couples of all ages—people of so many races gathered together. Just as Hope had prepared her, the women were dressed up in ways Charity would never describe as plain. The men were in everything from business suits to blue jeans. Some of the ladies wore fancy hats, while others left their heads uncovered. Still, there was something that seemed to set these people apart from the masses she'd seen before in Manhattan. It was the smiles on their faces.

A pianist began to softly play. Myrna stepped in front as a large Gospel Choir emerged and began to encircle the altar. There was Ivan, among them. It didn't take long for him to find them, too, judging from the wave he sent their way. Should she wave back? She pressed the backs of her fingers to her chin, then wiggled them discreetly. Ivan grinned broadly in return.

Charity exchanged a look with Aunt Hope. She waved back at Ivan, too, but with a pleasant reserve on her face. Going to the same church after breaking off a relationship must have its challenges. They would both have to forget themselves and remember why they were there.

A violinist joined the piano. Her face aglow, Myrna began to sing. She had heard Myrna sing before, but never quite so soulfully.

"Joyful, joyful we adore thee,
God of glory, Lord of love..."

With a flourish from the drums, the entire orchestra came alive; the tempo increased. The choir began to hum behind Myrna, swaying in time. Something seemed to spark across the congregation. Chills skittered across Charity's forearms. She glanced around her. Some people nodded, some lightly rocked left and right, mirroring the choir.

Charity felt Daniel slip his hand into hers. He hiked a congenial brow. It was certainly a new experience, for both of them. His gaze directed hers down to Aunt Hope's feet. She was tapping her toes to the beat, right along with the rest of them.

Merrily, Myrna called out to the congregation. "So, tell me. Are you feeling joyful this morning?"

Though there was just a light smattering in response, Myrna persisted. "Come on, now. Wake up, Sleepyheads. I'm gonna give you another chance. Are you feeling joyful?"

This time, all around them, congregants shouted back enthusiastically. Surprisingly, Aunt Hope was one of them. Charity exchanged a look with Daniel. It was hard to know exactly what to do. Should she just watch and listen?

Myrna turned to the choir as the orchestration swelled. "Choir, help me now! Put those hands together. Let's bring some of that Christmas joy to the world."

Daniel gave her hand a light squeeze as the choir began to clap in rhythm. No one up there clapped with more abandon than Ivan. It wasn't just the choir, though. The whole congregation was picking up the cadence, too. Myrna spoke in time. Congregants began to call out things like "come on" and "bring it" and "that's right." Not even Bethany had told her about a church quite like this. It was unlike anything she'd experienced in a lifetime of Sundays at home.

Before she knew it, Myrna gestured toward them. "Now, we've got some friends here today," she began.

Heat crawled up Charity's neck, into her cheeks. The weight of a thousand eyes pressed upon her.

Aunt Hope draped an affectionate arm around her shoulders. Charity returned a grateful smile. *She understands.*

"Now, this young couple over here," Myrna continued, "they're from Hope's people. They might dress a little different, but they're still very much a part of our family of faith. The thing about the Amish is, they know how to raise a barn. That's right. All them get together. They're good to each other. They help one another out."

Quite sure her face was scarlet, Charity shot a sheepish grin at Daniel.

"So, let's go on and do our own version of that," Myrna went on, "just to make them feel at home. Ain't no room to raise a barn in here. Uh-uh. So instead, how 'bout we just raise the roof, all right? Because between you and me, Brother and Sister-friends, I hear the thing ain't on too tight."

Shouts from the congregation increased as the orchestra swelled. The choir burst into jubilant song:

*"Joy to the world, the Lord is come
Let earth receive her King!"*

The carol was familiar, but never had Charity heard it sung with anywhere near this kind of exuberance. Let alone with harmonies or all those instruments. It was infectious, really. Aunt Hope was caught up immediately. She shot a nod Charity's way, welcoming her to add her voice to the throng.

Could I? Should I?

Charity checked Daniel. He was taking it all in very quietly. What would he think if she went along with anything outside of their traditions?

"Let every heart prepare Him room..." They sang those words like they really meant them. And for the first time, she really heard them.

Every heart. Not just Amish hearts. Not just English. Their hearts, my heart, united in spirit. Tentatively, Charity opened her mouth. The moment she did, a gentle effervescence enveloped her. What was that? Everything inside her shimmered. From the top of her head, to the tips of her toes. She closed her eyes and drank it in deeply. *Oh, dear Gott... You're here. You really are here, too.*

This was worship. It truly was, in an entirely new light. No, it wasn't like anything she'd ever experienced among the Amish. But suddenly, the truth dawned on her, like whispers on the wind: it was the birth of the very same Savior they celebrated. And somehow, in the midst of it all, she could not help but sing.

nine

Leanne's ankles throbbed. In some ways, she was torn about calling in sick again. It was always harder to face work on Sundays, when Hope had the day off. The Sunday crew wasn't nearly as patient with her. *Motivate*, she coaxed herself. She felt herself drifting off again. Dreamland beckoned. Frank could call in a temp.

Sleeping in sure beat standing on her aching feet for hours on end. It had it all over scouring pots and pans. She opened her eyes and stared at the ceiling. There was definitely a downside to taking the sick day, too. It meant she'd be alone, rattling around in Hope's apartment.

Smokey meowed at her feet.

"Sure. Now you like me."

As aloof as the cat had been when she'd tried to make friends, apparently, come feeding time, Smokey knew no strangers.

Leanne put the pillow over her head.

Smokey kept on meowing. It wasn't a contented sort of one-syllable mew meant as a greeting. That, she could blow off easily enough. Nope. These were back-to-back, impossibly elongated, ear-twisting *meeee-owwwws*. Smokey was demanding attention.

How was she supposed to ignore all that racket? Hope must have already fed her, before they'd all left for church. It had been nice enough of Hope to invite her to go with them, but please. The last thing she wanted was to darken the door of a house of worship, not in her condition. Just the thought of that gave her the shivers. As royally as she'd messed up, keeping as low a profile with God and the world as possible was the best way to go this Christmas.

Leanne thought back over the years of Christmases at home. Christmas was a time when the child in her mother really came out of hiding. It was insane the way her mom always got such a kick out of decorating and baking.

Momma King also took gift-wrapping to an almost ludicrous new level. There were coded tags with different characters' names on all the packages each year. No one in their family could ever figure out whose gift was whose before sun-up on Christmas day.

Last year, the gifts had all been tagged with the Wise Men's names. She thought she'd cracked the code, but wrong again, Dingbat. As it had turned out, she'd gotten all three wrong. She was Balthazar. Jay-Jay was Melchior, and Dad was Caspar.

Leanne smirked. When she was ten, she'd succeeded at sneaking a peek downstairs in the wee hours of Christmas morning. (It wasn't so hard to get up then, when she wasn't the size of an elephant seal.) Even then, tiptoeing down there would've been a lot easier without that creaky step near the bottom. Still, she'd made it.

By flashlight, she'd leaned in close to the Christmas tree. She'd read all the clues to decipher Momma's goofy gift-tagging code, dangling with the tinsel in front of her. That year, she wasn't Elizabeth Bennet or even her older sister Jane. She was Mr. Darcy. They were all characters from this dusty old Jane Austen novel Momma loved to read over and over. Anyway, once she knew which gifts were hers, she'd ventured to open the most enticing box of all. It was a sleek little razor scooter. Jackpot.

Sneaking an advance peek had only worked that one year. Then, wouldn't you know it? Her parents got wise. The following Christmas, she had found her door completely booby-trapped. A precarious pile of broomsticks, lampshades, and wooden chairs had come clattering down, just as soon as she'd turned her doorknob. What a racket that made! Of course, her misadventure had been memorialized by her dad on video. No way she'd ever live that one down.

Would there be coded packages under the tree for her this Christmas? Leanne couldn't help but wonder. But then again, knowing her parents, she was sure of the answer. Momma and Daddy would never give up. The tree would still be up and waiting, with all of her gifts under it, when she returned home after the baby.

Being away at Christmas sure wasn't easy, not the way she ached to see her family. But that was just it. There was no way she could bear what going home would do to them. It hung like a humongous rock around her neck. It set that familiar taunt-fest off all over again.

Seriously. How could she disappoint them by letting them see her this way? It would be hardest of all to face Daddy. How could she, after making that pledge to him that she'd wait until she was married, just like he and Momma had? How could she embarrass them like this, in front of the rest of the family and every last one of their friends? Forget about even trying to look Jaybird in the eye. Not after what she'd done. Radically humiliating. That's what it was.

Smokey was no help. She continued to throw a kitty-fit. It wore at her nerves, like a little kid who refused to stop pestering. In a weird way, it kind of reinforced her decision. She'd have to put her baby up for adoption. Absolutely.

It hadn't been very often that she'd toyed with the idea of keeping the baby. Not at all. For one thing, keeping the baby would mean telling her family what she'd done. Even beyond that, why would she want the responsibility of getting up to nurse a wailing infant? She hardly had the energy to scrape herself up to feed Hope's cat.

And as if Smokey's wall-to-wall pleas weren't disturbing Leanne's peace enough, Hope's telephone started ringing in counterpoint. She stuck her fingers in her ears. The machine would pick it up eventually. Still, there was Smokey, pawing at her foot, refusing to be outlasted.

Groggily, Leanne sat up. "Okay, okay. I'll get you something. Just give me a minute." Wearily, Leanne rose and shuffled toward the kitchen.

After about a half a dozen rings, Hope's answering machine did, in fact, click on. A young guy's voice sounded over the speaker.

"This message is for Hope Bright. It's Sean, from the agency. I'll try your cell, too. You have a callback tomorrow for 'Weather Eye.' That's Monday, noon, same stage, same role, same everything, but be prepared to sing this time. Break a leg."

Whatever.

Leanne opened the refrigerator. Neatly stacked by Hope's tip jar was a slender tower of cat food cans. She pulled the first one off the top. Liver flavor. *Barf-o-rama.* Maybe tuna. She swapped it out. Fish didn't seem all that much better.

As she set the can down to weigh the decision, she couldn't help but let her eyes wander. There was Hope's tip jar. The thing was almost three quarters full. It had to weigh a ton.

How much must that be in there?

She pressed her lips together as she stared at it. Here was the thing: Hope had said she could help herself to anything in the refrigerator. Sure, Hope probably meant food and drink, but what about the prenatal vitamins that she'd run out of last week? Vitamins were kind of like food, she reasoned. They were nourishment, to make the baby inside her stronger. A practically unnoticeable number of quarters from that jar could get her what she needed. She bit at the side of her cheek. It was like her hand was a magnet, being drawn toward that jar. She reached in, pulled it out, and shut the fridge.

Smokey yowled louder than ever.

Leanne unscrewed the lid. "You hush, Smokey. I'll feed you soon enough." Smokey tipped her head at her. "I can pay it back. Besides, I ain't takin' all that much. She won't even miss it."

Skaters whirled around the ice at the foot of the Rockefeller Center Christmas tree. Something in Charity bubbled up at the sight. Young and old, colorfully bundled, they circled in celebration of the season. As hardened as so much of the city seemed to such old-fashioned pleasures, this particular pastime was refreshing.

While Charity laced her skates, Daniel sat beside her, busying himself with his carving. He really was putting some time into it. The form of a small horse was beginning to emerge from his block of oak. It would make a nice gift.

Aunt Hope looped a bow on her skates, then rose to her feet. She glanced at Daniel. "Sure you don't want to try?"

Daniel waved her off with a smile. "No, no. The taller the man, the harder the fall. You two go right ahead."

Charity steadied herself on the rail as she stood on the ice. The blades seemed so thin. Tentatively, she slid a foot forward. *Whoa.* The kids made it look easy. If they could do it, she could learn. She braved another uncertain step.

Aunt Hope quickly extended a gloved hand. "I've got you." Together, they waited for a break in the crowd of skaters. Aunt Hope's breath crystallized into puffs of vapor. "All this time I've lived in New York City, watched them light the tree, watched the skaters, and I've never once set foot on this ice. First time for everything, right?"

Charity's jaw dropped. "You don't skate?"

Aunt Hope shrugged. "How hard can it be? You hold me. I'll hold you, and poof, we're skating."

"Ohhh-kay." Charity grasped her aunt's hand, and together they wobbled onto the ice. Taking a last look back at Daniel, she couldn't help notice a familiar face approaching. Ivan. He seated himself on the bench beside Daniel.

"Uh-oh," Hope murmured to Charity.

"Did you know Ivan was coming?"

"Not exactly. I'd kind of mentioned doing this. But it was before I broke it off with him." Aunt Hope turned back toward the ice.

"Did you want to skate with him instead?" Charity asked.

"Nope."

"Sure?"

Aunt Hope took her arm definitively. "I think I'd rather share this little first with you." She led her forward, onto the ice.

Hand in hand, they slid, just one gawky stride at a time at first. Quickly, Charity made a discovery: it helped to raise her free arm to the side. She whirled it around a time or two to regain her balance. Staying upright on that slender blade sure was heart-pounding, but in a very good way. Who knew it would be such fun to chase away her fears and just do something that scared her? Aaron and Isaac would be so jealous when they heard. Bethany, too.

Before long, they were gliding along almost respectably, if Charity didn't say so herself. If one started to slip, the other would help keep the two of them steady. With both of them working it out together, they were doing a lot better than she would have guessed, actually. They blended in with moms and dads, children, couples in love. There were even a few very talented skaters, jumping and spinning as they circled the rink.

Charity relished the crisp air on her face. It was pretty close to idyllic. This was Christmas in New York City. And in the secret place of her heart, she liked it.

"Whoa!" Aunt Hope shouted.

Charity snapped to attention. It couldn't be, but it was.

A rambunctious teenager, skating upstream, was barreling straight toward them.

It happened so quickly, too quickly to get out of his way. Before she knew it, they were going down. The ice was hard and wet when they hit.

Skaters swerved around them. Charity bruised nothing but her pride, but as she started to sit up, she realized that Aunt Hope had fared worse. She was cradling her left wrist, wincing in pain.

Charity scanned the emergency room's waiting area. Nearly every seat was filled. No sooner than one person left, another would arrive to fill the empty space. Finally, a spot opened up beside Daniel. Ivan slid into it. Daniel had offered Ivan his chair, but Ivan had insisted that Daniel and Charity should be seated first. She rubbed her hands across her skirt. Now that Ivan was right beside them, the pauses in conversation were all the more awkward.

Charity took in the English around her. Young and old, parents, and singles of many races and descriptions united in one activity: watching the clock, hoping for word about their loved ones. Many of them—children included—passed the time by talking or tapping on electronic devices of one kind or another. Others sat silently, worry etched on their faces.

Ivan leaned forward in his seat. "Are you sure you do not want an X-ray, Charity?"

"Yes. Thank you, Ivan. I'm fine." She crossed her ankles under her chair. Ivan was nice enough. He seemed legitimately concerned about Aunt Hope. Then, why was it so hard to get comfortable with his presence there?

Charity searched her soul. Perhaps it was because Aunt Hope had ended things between them. Then again, maybe she was hesitant about Ivan because of the sway he might have with Aunt Hope. The timing of their breakup sure had seemed providential. But what if he worked his way back into her life? Whatever remained of their relationship could hold Aunt Hope back. It could keep her from wanting to return with them this Christmas. Charity shifted in her seat. Was she completely selfish to even think that way?

Ivan turned to Daniel. "So, how do you like it here in the city?"

Daniel tipped his head. "It's not like home."

Ivan nodded thoughtfully. "I suppose that is why I like it." Again, silence. He turned toward Charity. "Did you enjoy the service this morning?"

"Oh, yes," Charity replied. "Very much."

Ivan glanced back at Daniel. "There was never a church like that where I come from. Let me tell you something. It is a very special thing to be able to share your faith with your kin. And so openly."

"It is," Daniel agreed. "Your family...do they believe as you do?"

"I have a few brothers in that way, but no relatives," Ivan said. "I was an orphan. We did not have much. But there is good in everything, you see. That is where I learned English, in the orphanage. It was from a Russian-English Bible an old woman used to read to us boys when no one else was looking. They caught her one day. They threw the Bible into the fireplace and dragged her away from us. It was the last time we saw her, but we got the Bible back out before it had burned too much. We taped it inside another book's cover and hid it. There was a place under a loose board in the floor. And we kept on reading the stories to each other in secret, whenever we could. We read it and talked about it in English, so even if they overheard, they could not understand what we were saying. No one ever adopted us, but Sergei, Anton, and I...we adopted each other."

Charity tucked her arms around her middle. She had been so wrong to think of Ivan as she had. What must that have been like for him to grow up that way, with no blood relations at all?

She was reluctant to pry, but a story played across Ivan's face. It was a tale of a very difficult childhood in a foreign land, a bitter place he'd struggled to survive and escape to this country. It took her back across the centuries, all the way to the persecution that made her Amish ancestors flee their homes in Europe to find refuge in America. It was so bewildering to think that their forefathers had been drowned, starved, beheaded, sometimes burned at the stake—all for nothing more than their convictions about baptism, the same baptism that she would soon freely receive.

"Charity Bright?"

Charity looked up. The wait was finally over. She rose to her feet.

A nurse approached in brightly printed attire. "Your aunt asked if you'd come sit with her."

Charity turned back to Daniel. "Are you all right waiting here for me?"

"As long as it takes," he promised.

Ivan sidled up to the nurse. "Is she okay?"

The nurse nodded reassuringly. "She'll be fine." She turned to Charity and extended a cordial arm, directing her toward the hall. "Right this way."

The nurse's shoes squeaked every step along the shiny hallway floor.

Charity stole a glance through each door they passed. There were so many signs of technology, advancements that were completely foreign to her way of life. She eyed the flashing lights. Intermittent beeps and clicks sounded from various devices they passed. What did all of those machines do? Charity couldn't help wonder. Was it wrong to be curious about such things?

A priest in a black suit with a starched white collar greeted her in passing. The man addressed the nurse by name. He must be a regular visitor here, she supposed. Apparently, he was a man of faith. He seemed so comfortable in this setting. So, why couldn't she be?

The nurse slowed at a partitioned area, then pulled back a curtain. There was Aunt Hope, sitting on something between a bed and an adjustable chair, an ear to her cell phone. It was impossible not to notice Aunt Hope's dismay as she lowered the phone and hit a button. A sharp chirp sounded.

Aunt Hope shook her head in disbelief. "Hi."

Charity hadn't seen such a downcast look since she'd been there. She moved to the side of the bed. "Are you in pain?"

"Some, but it's not my wrist. It's... Well, I just checked my messages." Hope pocketed the phone. "I got a call—a callback actually. This is the first one ever for a real Broadway play, and here, they're putting me into a cast. Not the cast-cast, meaning in the play cast, no. We're talking big honking Plaster-of-Paris up to my elbow type cast."

Charity's face fell. "It's broken."

"Fractured," Aunt Hope replied. "Story of my life." Something like grief weighed on her face.

Plays weren't something Charity knew much about, but seeing how disappointed Aunt Hope was, Charity's heart went out to her. "Maybe you could still be in the play. Maybe they wouldn't mind."

Hope sighed. "No, it's...you know what? Maybe it's for the best. Goldie would say I was just compensating, but...truth is, if I had to choose between doing that play and having the time with you, Charity..." A fond look brightened her. "Well, that's what we here in the city call a no-brainer."

Charity gently brushed Aunt Hope's shoulder. "Still hurts, though. Doesn't it?"

"Some, but...nothing like all these years without you, without my family."

Privately, Charity thanked Gott. A door had opened. "I can't imagine what it's been like all these years, to be shunned."

Soberly, Aunt Hope shook her head. "Afraid not. Not till it's you."

Charity pulled up a chair and sat. "I couldn't do it. Already, I miss everyone so much. I don't know how you do it."

A bittersweet smile crossed Hope's face. "You know, when I was getting my X-ray—you know what an X-ray is, right?"

Charity nodded. "My friend, Bethany had one in town when she got bronchitis. Ivan was just asking if I wanted one."

Aunt Hope shifted her lips to the side. "He's still here, huh?"

"So he is."

"Well, anyway, while I was in there having my X-ray, I was thinking about your mamm."

The thought warmed Charity. "You were?"

Regret glimmered in Aunt Hope's eyes. "I'm telling you, Charity. If she could have had just a spoonful of the medical attention I've had today... I guess it's hard to know for sure. But I'm thinking she'd probably still be with us."

Charity's breath caught in her throat. Her mind whirled. "Wait." Maybe it would discourage Aunt Hope from returning with her. Even so, Charity had to pursue it. "You don't think Mamm had to die?"

"I really don't." Hope cradled her injured arm.

It was hard to know what to say after that, but it seemed like she should at least try. "We're making progress, you know." Charity held Aunt Hope's dubious gaze. "Not so much our family, but a few of the others are. Since Bethany's Uncle Caleb became one of the ministers, there have been a few changes. Most still have their babies at home, but a lot of people go to English doctors in town for other things, especially when it's serious."

Aunt Hope nodded. "That's good."

Charity smiled. "Of course, the old wood stove keeps the kitchen plenty warm, but we heat the rest of the house with propane."

Wryly, Aunt Hope straightened. "Now, there's a quantum leap."

"I know that's not so very much, but there are bigger things. Like there's power equipment for farming. More and more community phones in little shanties here and there. Some people have cell phones for business."

"Anything your Dat lets you use?"

"Dat let me come here."

Aunt Hope eyes tightened. Clearly, her wheels were turning. "He wants me to come home, doesn't he?"

Caught. Charity could only admit the truth. "*Ja*, well... We all do." When Aunt Hope averted her eyes, Charity took hold of her good hand. "Think of it, Aunt Hope. We could cook and exchange gifts and sing carols this Christmas. We could all be a family again. Can you imagine how happy Opa would be?"

Aunt Hope wistfully raised her brows. "I have imagined it. I imagine it all season, leading up to every single Christmas. Even dream of it sometimes. I go back and forth, convincing myself, then talking myself out of it. It's why I broke it off with Ivan. It's why I never married. How can I commit to life here when my heart is still so torn?"

Charity ached.

What must it have been like for Aunt Hope, all these years alone, caught between the English and Amish worlds? Everything that Dat had said about the purpose of shunning came flooding back. Indeed, it was plain to see that Aunt Hope missed her family, maybe enough to draw her home.

Charity gazed at Daniel as they perused the city produce market's bountiful array of fresh fruit and vegetables. Even everyday tasks like this were a delight with him at her side. Daniel dutifully carried a shopping basket as she selected green beans. An onion to sauté, a couple of red tomatoes, and some toasted almond slivers would complete Oma's family recipe.

"You know, Daniel, I really think there's a chance Aunt Hope will come."

Daniel turned, pleased. "Did she say so?"

Charity tied off the top of the bag of beans. In a way, she hesitated to divulge too much. Aunt Hope had entrusted her with what had surely been guarded truths. She had best respect her privacy. "She said she's torn."

Daniel held out the basket for Charity. "Perhaps the aroma of Amish-made supper will help."

"I thought that very thing." She picked up a curious looking piece of fruit. Never had she seen anything like it before, even during day-trips to the market in town. It was yellow and oblong, with funny little reddish spikes all around. Intrigued, she sniffed its rind. "Have you ever seen so many kinds of fruit? I don't even know what this is. And the size of the apples. Here it is December and—"

"You make a fine apple butter with what we grow, Charity."

It was hard not to blush. "Well, thank you, Daniel. I like that you noticed. Dat eats it, but he never says a word."

Daniel turned his gaze casually. "He has to me."

Charity dropped her chin. "About my apple butter?"

"Among other things."

"Is it entirely immodest of me to ask what?" Charity bagged a large onion.

Daniel made some space in the basket to accommodate her find. "He tells me that you sew and cook, that you tend to the house. All quite well. He said that you raised your brothers, just as if they were your own." A sly expression curved on Daniel's lips. "One would think he was trying to make a match of us."

Oh, my.

Masking her delight, Charity considered Daniel's words. "And would such a match please you?"

"Very much," Daniel confessed. "If it would please you."

His eyes were searching hers.

She knew it.

Though she feigned to mull the idea over, she allowed a demure smile to wander across her lips. "Well, then. Perhaps we should consider it."

Hope struggled to find the keys to her building. A pristine white cast encased her left arm, from the base of her fingers, nearly to her elbow. Rooting around in her purse wasn't easy, using only her right hand.

Ivan jockeyed for position. "Would you please let me help you with that?"

What was she supposed to say? The truth was, she didn't want to need help. At least, not from Ivan. "I've got six weeks with this thing," she reminded. "Might as well figure out how to work with my right hand." She continued to fumble. "You know, my family tried to break me of being a lefty. Thought it was somehow bad or... Okay, if you can just find the keys in there, maybe I can—"

Gently, Ivan took the purse from her. "There. I have it." He set the bag on the capstone of the stair rail. Systematically, he began to remove its contents.

Hope fidgeted. How could any woman be comfortable with her ex going through her purse? Not that there was anything in there a grown man hadn't seen before. But still.

"Is it so hard for you to need someone?"

Hope exhaled. This was frustrating. He was not going to make this easy. "I never said I didn't need anyone."

Ivan pulled out her wallet and set it down. "Not in so many words. But you are pushing me away."

"No, Ivan. You were pushing me. It was all too fast. There's a difference."

Ivan raised his hands. "So, I stop pushing. I am just here."

Hope drew her open coat around her middle. "For the next month or so. Shouldn't you be out speed dating or something?"

Ivan shook his head as he fished her keys from her bag. No doubt, he had caught her drift. He dangled her keys before her, holding her gaze. "If a month is all the time I have left, I choose to spend that month with you."

ten

It was ironic, really. At least Charity thought so. There they were in Aunt Hope's New York City apartment—right in the middle of the English world—but you would never have known it based on what the four of them were doing that evening. There was no television set on, no clacking of a computer keyboard, not even a cell phone in use. Oddly, it was as if they were back home, enjoying the homespun activities of Amish Country.

As she let down the hem of the waitress uniform Frank had said she'd have to wear, Daniel fine-tuned the carving on his horse and buggy toy for his brother. Leanne sat nearby, doing a very nice job of painting holly on Aunt Hope's new white cast. Hope curled up under one of her quilts, sipping a cup of hot cider.

Leanne dipped her brush into scarlet paint, then dotted it to add berries between the prickly green leaves. The plaster of the cast drank in the vibrant paint colors readily. Leanne glanced sidelong at Charity. "I don't see why you're lettin' that hem down. If you ask me, you'd get a lot better tips leavin' it shorter."

And suddenly, they were back in Manhattan.

Charity continued to whipstitch the lengthened hem. "Maybe, but...well, I guess I'm just more comfortable with it this way."

Hope observed Leanne's artistry on her cast. "You watch. I'll fill that tip jar in no time with this baby. Serving up the tea, raking in the sympathy."

Leanne blew the paint dry. "How you gonna write your orders?"

"Not sure. Right-handed scrawl, I guess," Hope countered.

Leanne scooted closer. "I knew a guy once who could write with his toes."

"Quite a talent, but...." Hope admired her cast. "See, now, I think you've been holding out on me."

Strange. If Charity hadn't been looking right at Leanne, she might well have missed it. But an almost guilty look flickered across Leanne's face.

"What do you mean?" Leanne scowled.

Hope smiled broadly. "Look how you can paint. And completely freehand. You're really good."

Leanne dipped her brush back into the paint. She seemed to relax again. "Last spring, me and

Reggie painted the backdrop for our school play. Did the whole thing by our lonesomes, up real late and all. It's kinda how I got this whole beached whale look goin'."

English girls sure didn't hold back. Charity exchanged a glance with Daniel. Conversation was quite a bit more frank in the city, she supposed. From the expression on Daniel's face, she could tell that he agreed.

It wasn't so much that situations like this didn't occur among the Amish. Charity had known more than one girl who had taken the license of Rumspringa and found herself in Leanne's condition. Like Daniel's cousin, Lydia. Pregnancy just wasn't something they really talked about, at least not so openly. Never in mixed company.

Hope scratched under the end of her cast. "This Reggie...he's the guy?"

Leanne shrugged. "Yeah, but...he don't know it. Never paid no mind to me after that night anyways. Daddy didn't like the looks of him from the start. So, he was just as glad we quit hangin' out. My parents are way old-school that way, you know? They don't get it that nobody waits anymore."

Hope cut a glance at Charity and Daniel. "Some people still wait."

Leanne rolled her eyes. "I mean normal people. No offense, but can we just put it on the table here that the whole Amish dealio is a little behind the beat? Kind of out there?"

Hope shot Leanne a reproving look. "Leanne..."

"Well, it is," Leanne blurted. "I betcha good money right here and now that the two of you, you probably haven't even kissed."

Charity felt a blush rise to her cheeks. She ventured a look at Daniel. How would he respond?

Hope leaned toward Leanne. "That's kind of not our business."

Daniel took Leanne's comment in stride. "There's nothing that says that Amish couples can't kiss during Rumspringa."

Leanne's eyes narrowed. "Rum what?"

"Rumspringa. That's what we're on, now," Daniel explained. "Before we commit to being Amish, we're allowed to experience the world."

Leanne took it in, a smirk forming. "So, are you saying that you two have experienced the world of kissing?"

Daniel glanced Charity's way. A shy twinkle lit in his eyes. "I'm saying that what does or doesn't happen between Charity and me...it's up to Charity and me to decide when we'd like to share it."

Charity breathed a contented sigh. Daniel was so discreet. It also hadn't escaped her notice that he'd referred to them as a couple. Indirectly, at least. Myrna had called them a couple in front of the whole congregation that morning, but now Daniel had. She turned the idea over in her mind as she unwound a new length of thread, her heart warming with a memory. "You make me think of Dat, Leanne. That's what I call my father. When I was little, Dat taught me how to make this pie. It's so sweet and smells so good that they call it Shoo-fly Pie."

Leanne scrunched her brow. "And this applies to my smoochin' question exactly how?"

Charity snipped her thread from the spool. "When it comes to private subjects, Dat has this way of talking about one thing when he really means something else."

Aunt Hope snickered. "You noticed that, too?"

Nimbly, Charity threaded her needle, knotting the end with one hand. "First pie I made, Dat had me serve, piping hot, right alongside the cabbage and smoked turkey we were having. You know how cabbage smells, and I could hardly even get a whiff of the turkey. But that pie...it has all this gooey dark molasses and brown sugar. And the aroma of that pie, it wafted right over everything else on the table."

Aunt Hope inhaled. "Sounds heavenly."

Charity sighed, recalling the aroma. "Of course, Dat, he saw me eyeing that piece of pie. He told me it was my choice. I could eat it first, if I wanted. I admit I started to, but when I was just about to take a bite, he got that little smile Dat sometimes gets. You know, Aunt Hope?"

"Sure do," she smiled.

Charity resituated the uniform. "Anyway, what Dat told me was that the pie would taste even sweeter if I saved it for the right time."

Aunt Hope nodded with recognition. "Same way Oma introduced 'the talk' to Nathan and me. Only it was rhubarb pie. Nathan was very big on rhubarb."

Charity glowed. "Still is."

Leanne kept on painting, a vexed expression wrinkling on her lips. "Well, you know, your whole waitin' bit, that's real folksy and all, but I still think it's weird."

Mercifully, silence reigned. What more could be said? What a relief to just return to her hemming. With each stitch, Charity continued to ruminate on the conversation. Daniel certainly had been quick to state his view that kissing was permissible during Rumspringa. Yes, he had held her hand—more than once, now—but he had not so much as grazed her cheek with his lips. There had certainly been plenty of opportunity, but he had not taken it.

She stole a glance at his face. What would it be like if he ever expressed his heart to her in that way? Would he ask first? Would he simply draw her close? How it would come to be, she didn't know. The only thing she was certain of was that she was finally allowing herself to feel that pull of desire.

Charity helped Aunt Hope dab her face dry with a soft terry towel. Even simple tasks presented a new challenge with only one good arm to use.

"Guess I'll have to get the hang of doing all kinds of things right-handed," Aunt Hope supposed. She attempted to hang the damp towel on the bathroom bar. "Sorry about that whole inquisition in there. I know how it feels to be put on the spot."

Charity reached over to help pull the towel through for her. "It's okay. I'm not ashamed of who we are."

Aunt Hope caught Charity's eye in the mirror. "I guess the truth is that I have been. Not ashamed so much as... I don't know. I've only hinted about it to Ivan. Must be some reason I never told people out here who I was."

Charity turned away from the mirror to Aunt Hope's face. "You say *was*. But it's still who you are, Aunt Hope. You're still a part of us. That is, if you want to be."

Aunt Hope leaned against the bathroom counter thoughtfully. "With you here, I feel that, but most of the time, especially at this time of year, it's... I'm like Leanne said. I'm kind of out there."

It pained her to see the bittersweet sadness in Aunt Hope's eyes, but in a way, Charity thanked Gott for it. It provided the opening she needed. She could finally say what had been rumbling around in her mind all evening. "You know, I saw some rhubarb at the market today. It's out of season for us, so Dat would never expect it. But we could surprise him for Christmas dinner."

Aunt Hope lit up. "You would take it to him for me?"

Ever so gently, Charity thought. "Well, I could, and I would, but... Oh, Aunt Hope, just think how much better it could be if we took it to him. Together."

Aunt Hope drew back. "Oh, wow. Wouldn't that be amazing?" Chagrinned, she held up her brightly painted cast. "Of course, this cast isn't exactly the plainest thing."

Charity's heart swelled. Clearly, Aunt Hope was actually entertaining the idea. "Can you imagine their faces if we rode up together with his favorite pie? And Opa...Opa would cry he'd be so thrilled."

Aunt Hope's face slowly fell. "Ah, Charity... Honey, it's—"

Charity quickly raised a hand. "Don't say no, yet. Please. Just wait. Give it time. Think about it."

Aunt Hope dropped her head. "Okay, but—"

"Promise me. Just that you'll think."

Aunt Hope seemed to ponder it skeptically. "Just think."

"Just live with the idea for a while yet," Charity suggested.

As Daniel piled a stack of linens on the sofa, Charity dropped to her knees. A few of his curly wood shavings had fallen to the floor.

Daniel tucked a pillow into a cotton case. "I'll get that."

"It's no bother."

"I know," Daniel answered. "That's one of the things I love about you."

What did he just say?

Tossing the shavings into a waste can, Charity let Daniel's words echo in her mind. Saying that he loved things about her was not so very far from saying that he loved her. She nudged him playfully. "One of the things?"

Daniel set the pillow aside. He sat on the sofa and patted the cushion beside him. "I suppose there are others yet."

Charity eased onto the sofa beside Daniel. "You suppose?"

"I suppose." Daniel put a finger to his lips, then took Charity's hand. "Come with me."

"Now? Where?"

Daniel led Charity to Hope's door. He grabbed her cape off the hook and draped it around her shoulders. "Shhh... I want to show you something."

Hand in hand, Daniel led Charity up the two additional flights of stairs to the top of the building. Her heart rose with each step, as light as a feather. Where was he taking her?

"I found this earlier, while you were making supper." Daniel opened the steel door on the upper landing, and led her out to the flat rooftop. "Okay, use your imagination. Look past the air conditioner. And beyond the electrical box there. Look way up, above all the buildings and the city lights. Pretend the glow is...like it's a reflection of what's above it. Just look up, at the stars."

Charity took into the crisp night air. She tilted her face up to drink in the twinkling heavens. "*Ja*, well... Look at that. Same sky, huh?"

"So it is."

"It's almost like we're back where we belong."

Daniel returned an inviting smile. "That's what I thought, too." He brushed back a lock of hair that had escaped Charity's kapp. His fingers lingered on her cheek, so affectionately, before returning to his side.

Charity blushed. It was hard to know just what to say. "She's thinking about coming home with us, you know."

"Really?"

Charity nodded. "She promised. Just to think, but it's a start."

Daniel was visibly pleased. "That, it is."

Charity whispered with a conspiratorial chuckle. "I felt like Dat, putting the pie out in front of her. We'll just let her look at it for a while yet. Take in that scent of home."

Daniel stood silently for a moment, looking full into Charity's face. "You know what's home to me?"

"What?"

"You are, Charity. You have been for so long."

"Daniel..."

"Shhh..." Daniel took Charity's hand. Charity accepted it, savoring his touch. He looked down at their interlaced fingers, then back into her face. "It's not just that I love things about you, Charity. I love you. I think I always have."

Tears brimmed in Charity's eyes. Never had she heard words like this. She raised Daniel's hand to her face, and then brushed it with her lips.

It was impossible to miss the longing in his eyes.

"Dat was right," Charity smiled. "It's all the sweeter when you wait."

"Charity... We don't have to prove anything to any—"

Gently, Charity put a finger to his lips. "Shhh..." She stroked his handsome face. The sight of him took her breath away. Her heartbeat quickened as he quietly held her gaze.

To be sure, she had waited a long time for this moment. Now that it had come, it caught her completely by surprise. She'd always wondered how it would be, how she should receive something as intimate as a first kiss. Then, suddenly, at the deepest part of her, she found an undeniable desire to give that gift to him. Initiating didn't seem so Amish. No, not at all. But under the glorious starlight of Gott's heaven, it did feel completely right.

She searched Daniel's eyes. They were filled with that same longing she felt, but his posture remained respectful. He was waiting for her to be ready.

At the core of her being, she knew that she was.

Slowly, she drew Daniel close, and into an exquisitely tender kiss. Years of yearning poured from her. His lips were so receptive. So soft and expressive. It was almost...well, it was as if they were communicating in a language that neither of them had ever known. All sense of time vanished. When they parted, neither spoke. They just stood, washed in wonder, bathed in the glow of the night.

As Charity pulled back the covers, Aunt Hope marked her place in the play she was reading. With a shake of her head, she set it aside, rose from her chair, and flicked off the light.

Charity climbed into bed. "If you'd like to keep that lamp on to read, I don't mind."

Aunt Hope sat on the bed. "That's okay. I know how that play ends. Very Greek. And I suppose I have enough tragedy in my life."

Aunt Hope had definitely known tragedy. How difficult it must have been to lose her closest friend—Charity's own mother—in childbirth. "Dat always says that you cannot appreciate joy until you have shed many tears."

Aunt Hope ran her fingers along the holly on her cast. "Nathan knows what it's like to lose someone you've loved."

"He does." It was a truth Charity had long known. Even as early as it was in her relationship with Daniel, she couldn't imagine what it would be like to lose him, to know she would never see him again this side of eternity.

With her right hand, Aunt Hope set her alarm clock.

"Have you ever been in love, Aunt Hope?"

"Once or twice," Aunt Hope noted. "Sort of."

"Really?"

Aunt Hope set the clock back on the nightstand. "Ancient history now, but...there was this boy back home." She settled under the sheets.

"Amish?"

"Through and through. You probably know him. Joseph Glick."

Recognition gleamed in Charity's eyes. "Yes, he's very nice. He's a good friend of Dat's. Married to Constance. They have six children and, from the looks of it, another on the way."

Hope situated her pillow. "That's good. Good for them."

There was an unmistakable tinge of regret in Aunt Hope's voice. It made Charity feel bad that she'd asked at all. Had she touched an old wound? "I'm sorry, Aunt Hope. Does that hurt you?"

"No, no. Not anymore," Aunt Hope answered. "He started calling on Constance just before I left. Never knew how I felt. I left because of your mother, but...he's part of the reason I didn't hurry back. At least, at first he was. Then, by the time I was over him, I'd kind of fallen in love with life here. And that was that."

Charity curled over on her side. There was something so wonderful about being able to talk this way with another woman, especially since Bethany was so far away. Charity hesitated to pry, but Aunt Hope's openness encouraged her. There was so little she knew about her aunt, and so much more she wanted to know. "So, it wasn't Ivan...the second time."

Even in the moonlight, Charity could see a glint in Aunt Hope's eyes. She could hear the nostalgia in her voice.

"Well," Aunt Hope began, "maybe it could have been, but... I guess we'll never know."

The faint rumble of traffic continued. It was not so quiet there at night as it was at home. A car alarm wailed insistently.

Aunt Hope shook her head. "Goodnight, Charity."

"Goodnight, Aunt Hope."

Though they did their best to settle in, both of them remained wide-awake. With all that had just transpired, Charity could not stop thinking. Her mind reviewed those stolen moments with Daniel, over and over again. It was a secret that burned inside of her, longing to be shared. Quietly, she whispered. "I kissed him tonight."

Aunt Hope rolled back over on her side. "Just now? In there?"

A smile curled on Charity's lips. "He took me up to the roof to surprise me, but I think I was the one who surprised him."

"You kissed him?"

"So I did." Charity beamed. "Our secret, okay?"

"Always."

Charity felt the color rise to her cheeks. "Dat likes him as a match for me."

It was a while before Aunt Hope responded. "I understand why that's important. I do. But, Charity, tell me... Are you in love with him?"

"I am." It was the strangest thing. Though she hadn't realized it until that very moment, everything in Charity was sure. She was also certain that she wanted Aunt Hope to be the very first to hear it.

eleven

Hope swallowed hard. The Café Troubadour was humming with activity, and there she was, sporting that elbow-to-wrist cast. Normally, a horde of hungry patrons would be considered a very good thing, but on this particular day, it complicated matters. Frank would hardly take her injured wrist as good news. At least Charity and Daniel had come. Hopefully, that would offset the blow.

It didn't take Frank long to spot her. There was even a dash of sympathy as he shook his head. Any way you sliced it, her work would be compromised.

Hope glanced over at Shep as he played a piano intro for Myrna. She raised the microphone to sing:

"I heard the bells on Christmas Day,
Their old familiar carols play,
And wild and sweet the words repeat,
Of peace on earth good will to men..."

When she got back from hanging up her coat in the locker room, Frank was at the cash register. He was wrangling with a jammed tape. That wouldn't improve his mood, not on a day like this.

Silently, Hope sent up a prayer. It hadn't been the first time that morning, but she knew she could use all the help she could get.

Through the pass-through window, she spotted Daniel. He had already started scrubbing a pot, back in the kitchen. Such a hard worker. Amish, through and through.

Charity followed at a discreet distance behind her, wearing her lengthened uniform. Frank wouldn't be crazy about the kapp over Charity's bun, but he'd just have to deal with it.

Light applause came from the dining floor as Myrna's carol came to a close. No time like the present to approach Frank. She threw back her shoulders and ambled his way.

Frank fed a fresh tape into the register. He barely looked at her. "My condolences and whatnot, Hope. But did you notice we're into the holiday rush and you can't even tote a tray?"

Hope gathered the mangled tape and pitched it into the recycle bin. "I'll cover the counter and the register one-handed. Charity can take my tables."

"Our wait staff sings," Frank insisted. "No exceptions. I told you, Charity can help in the kitchen, but sorry, Hope. There are a lot of talented wannabes lined up for your job."

Hope shot a glance at Charity. For her sake, she wanted so much to make this work. She watched as Charity quietly took it upon herself to venture onto the restaurant floor.

Hope turned back to her boss. "Frank, please. We'll figure it out. Daniel is a great worker. He'll help keep the kitchen going for you."

Frank popped the side of the register back into place. "It's simple arithmetic, Hope. I can't pay three people to do one person's work. Let alone that the customers here expect their servers to entertain."

"Oh, come on, Frank. They'll love her. And she'll work for tips only."

Stubbornly, Frank headed back toward the kitchen. "Not if she don't sing."

Hope slumped. It seemed the battle was lost. Then, she heard the sound of a pure young voice, coming from the stage. Hope looked over, astonished. Charity stood at the microphone, tentatively at first, singing *a cappella*. Soon, Shep softly picked up the melody on the piano.

> *"Oh, little town of Bethlehem,*
> *How still we see thee lie,*
> *Above thy deep and dreamless sleep,*
> *The silent stars go by."*

Halfway through the kitchen door, Frank stopped in his tracks. Slowly, he turned back. Hope watched breathlessly as he scanned restaurant's service floor, monitoring his customers' faces.

Normally, chatter continued when other staffers sang. This time, conversations ceased. Diners turned in their seats. They were all rapt on Charity, especially Hope. She did glance toward the kitchen briefly, in time to see Daniel as he stepped to the pass-through window. His gaze was so intent. It was also impossible to read.

Sitting at the counter, Goldie shot a cynical smirk Hope's way. "Touching, but so not secular. Isn't there an ordinance against those kind of carols yet?"

Myrna stepped in to heat up his coffee. "Last time I checked, this was still a free country."

Hope pushed Goldie's grousing aside. There was something that felt almost holy to her about the moment. Clearly, the rest of their customers were feeling it, too. Some began to sing along. Hope instinctively found herself wandering to the stage, adding her rich alto to Charity's lilting soprano.

> *"Yet in thy dark streets shineth,*
> *The everlasting light,*
> *The hopes and fears of all the years,*
> *Are met in Thee tonight."*

Shep smiled as Hope joined Charity beside the piano, her voice blending with Charity's as only family could. By the second verse, it seemed the whole restaurant was singing along, swept up in the miracle of the moment.

Everything in Hope sang. There had always been something about music that lifted her spirit, but this was even more so. In reality, she was in New York City, standing on a small stage in a not so chichi café. But inside, where it really mattered, harmonizing with Charity transported her. It took her to that place where, for so many years, she'd desperately longed to be. It took her home.

Hope closed out the register for the evening. It had been quite a prosperous day. As the last café customer bade them goodnight, Daniel put chairs on top of tables. Frank swept. Gratefully, Frank hadn't griped about Leanne calling in sick again. Not even once. He also hadn't mentioned a preference for Daniel's work ethic, though it was pretty clear that he had one.

Myrna dumped the fishbowl of tips from the piano onto the counter in front of Hope and Charity. It was easily twice the usual.

Shep's guide dog led him by, on his way out for the night. "Sounds like you did alright."

Myrna grinned broadly. "Better than alright, Baby. Don't you worry. I'll put yours aside."

Shep tipped his hat. "Pleasure to play for you, Angels."

Hope gave him an affectionate pat. "Night, now."

"Thank you, Shep," Charity added.

Shep turned toward Charity with a little bow. "My privilege."

As Shep neared the door, Hope's gaze fell on Ivan. How long had he been standing there, outside in the cold, waiting? As soon as he caught her eye, he waved. *Ah, well,* she sighed. She gave him a subtle wave in return. This break wasn't shaping up to be anywhere near as clean as she'd anticipated.

Myrna sidled up to Hope. "Lookee who's here again. Thought you two broke up."

"So did I." Hope straightened the many bills they'd received so all of the George Washingtons faced the same way. Actually, not only were there a slew of Washingtons, there were also quite a few Lincolns and Hamiltons, even a Jackson or two. "Have you ever seen tips like this? Charity, this is not normal."

Myrna's expression confirmed it. With a wink at Hope, she emphasized her words. She wanted Frank to overhear. "And the way you two blend. Mmm-mm! That was some kind of yuletide moment."

Frank set his broom aside. "Yeah, yeah, yeah. I hear ya."

Hope dealt the tips out into four piles. "Admit it, Frank. She did great."

Frank grabbed his dustpan. "That she did." He glanced back and forth between Charity and Daniel. "Don't suppose the two of you can stay on past Christmas."

Myrna reared back. "Somebody slap me! Frank's feeling generous!"

Frank wagged a congenial finger Myrna's way. "Hush, woman, before I give 'em your job."

Hope threw an affectionate arm around Charity. "You staying on is a thought. Maybe we both have something to think about. Huh, Charity?" It had popped out before she'd really thought it through.

Daniel paused briefly.

He must have heard her, too. Would they even consider it? There was the answer in Charity's sweetly conflicted eyes.

Frank ambled toward the counter. "What do you say, there, Little Missy?"

Hope watched as Charity exchanged a look with Daniel. "Well, it's...Daniel and I—"

It wasn't long before Daniel stepped up behind Frank. "We appreciate it, Frank. But our families are expecting us home on the twenty-fourth. We can't stay."

Despite Daniel's intervention, Hope kept an eye on Charity.

Charity stepped to Daniel's side. "Frank, it's so kind of you to offer, but we can't."

Hope took it in with a bittersweet smile. What might Charity have said if Daniel had given her a chance to answer for herself?

Masking her disappointment, Hope went back to organizing their tips. She should just accept it, she coaxed herself. This was the way of the Amish. Women had little voice there. So often, they deferred to the men in their lives as Charity had. Just as she, herself, had in her youth.

It all seemed so long ago, like a far away dream...actually a very happy one. It hadn't been a bad childhood. Not at all. In fact, so much of it had been wonderful, almost idyllic. Going home would be an adjustment, just like moving to the city had been. There'd be plusses and minuses either way.

Maybe Charity was right. Maybe she should go back to Amish Country with them.

Then again, maybe not.

At first, it would be bliss to wrap her arms around those she'd missed so dearly, most of all her brother, Nathan, and her dear ageing father. But in time, the rush of excitement over her homecoming would settle into day-to-day Plain life. How would she feel then?

Here, in the English world, she'd found such liberty in her faith. For years, she had answered to no one except her heavenly Father. She kind of liked it that way. Even if, somehow, she could find love among the Amish, would she be able to be the kind of wife that an Amish man would expect? Hard to say. On the other hand, would she ever allow herself to marry a man outside the Amish community? That would be tantamount to a decision to never return.

As she watched Charity and Daniel work side-by-side, helping Frank to close up for the night, Hope was mightily torn. Time was ticking away. How could she go back with them? Yet how could she bear to watch them go home without her, knowing it would be the last she'd ever see of them?

Smokey meowed.

Leanne scowled at her. For a cat, she could certainly be a mouthy little beast. And exasperating. Let's not forget exasperating. Leanne unscrewed the lid on Hope's tip jar. "I gave you your dinner. What more do you want?"

Smokey kept on yowling.

"You're just a cat." Leanne searched through the pickle jar for quarters. They were all ice cold. She winced as something snagged within her abdomen.

Again with the cramps. "And anyway, it's not that much. Not like I need to explain to—"

Hearing the rattle of a key being inserted into Hope's door lock, Leanne quickly pocketed the quarters. She screwed the lid back onto the jar just as she heard the door swing open.

"Hello?" Charity called out.

"In here." Hurriedly, Leanne stashed the tip jar. She'd pretend to rummage through the leftovers in the open refrigerator. That wouldn't raise suspicion. "Just getting something to eat. Are you hungry?"

Daniel rounded the corner. "No, we're fine. Frank fed us."

Leanne leaned around the kitchen wall, her pulse racing. Good. Hope wasn't there. Just Charity, taking off that ridiculous looking bonnet of hers. How Charity could traipse around in public dressed like she did was completely beyond her. "So, where's Hope?"

Charity untied her cape. "Out front with Ivan."

Leanne closed the refrigerator door. Even the sight of food at this point turned her stomach. "I am so sick of being pregnant. Nothing looks good." She fought to control the racing of her heart. What she needed to do was to get back into her room where she could stash the coins she had taken. The things were icy, plus they made her pockets bulge way out from her hips. Just leave casually, she told herself.

But when she brushed the counter going by, the stolen quarters jangled loudly. She slapped her hands down to silence them.

Immediately, Leanne saw Daniel put it together. He knew. And he knew she knew he knew. Charity let out a little gasp. She knew, too. Continuing the charade was pointless. "Go ahead, tell on me," she spat. "Get me thrown out on the street to have this baby. That'll be Christmassy!" Angrily, she strode past them. She stalked into her room and slammed the door.

Just inside, Leanne's chest heaved. What was she going to do now? The world was crashing down around her. One thing she knew: it was humiliating enough to get busted by Mr. and Miss Righteous. But there was no way she could face Hope, too, not after all that Hope had done for her.

Tears threatened. She did her best to suck them back into her head, right into the ducts they came from. Failing, she wiped them on her sleeve, then slid the closet door open. There was that ugly nylon duffel bag of hers. That again. Fitfully, she began to pack.

A soft knock sounded at the door.

"Go away!" Leanne shouted.

The door opened. Charity slipped inside.

Great. Just what she needed. A religious nut to make her feel even guiltier than she already did. She stuffed what little she owned into the duffel bag. "Don't you judge me. You and your holier-than-thou boyfriend. Neither one of you has the first clue what it's like to live out in the real world."

Charity dropped her eyes. "You're right. We don't."

Leanne emptied her dresser drawer. "I knew the minute you two showed up my ticket was up here. Should have packed then. Saved myself the trouble."

"Leanne, please stop."

"Why? So you can preach to me all about stealin'? You think I don't know right from wrong? Here." Furiously, Leanne emptied her pockets onto the bed. "Take it!"

Charity stepped toward Leanne. "You can still put it back."

Leanne grabbed the last of her socks and stuffed them into her bag. "That much I can. But not what I already spent. Stupid prenatal vitamins are costin' me a stinkin' fortune."

Charity faced Leanne. She was maddeningly calm. "How much more did you use?"

"Maybe thirty bucks." Leanne splayed her fingers into her hair. "What's the difference?"

Charity reached into her pocket and pulled out a handful of bills. Leanne's jaw gaped. Charity counted out thirty dollars and placed it beside the newly stolen quarters.

Leanne churned. How much more frustrating could this get? The nicer Charity was, then tada! The more hideous it made her by comparison. "What am I supposed to do with all that?"

Charity put a gentle hand on Leanne's shoulder. "Accept it as my Christmas gift to you, then do whatever you choose." Charity left quietly. She closed Leanne's door behind her.

Bewildered, Leanne plopped down on the bed. Another cramp ripped through her belly. Perfect. Wincing, she tried to relax her muscles. The people on the Internet said that was supposed to help, and she supposed it did, a little. Still, try as she may, she knew that no amount of relaxation could get her out of the train wreck she'd made of her life.

The pain fading, Leanne ran her fingers across the stolen coins on the bed. They were still damp and frosty beneath her fingers. *What a mess.* She looked at her duffel bag beside her. Charity might be able to live with paying off her debt. But the question Leanne couldn't dodge was: how could she live with herself?

It seemed only fair to Hope that she should let Ivan walk her home from the café. That meant she'd had to ask Daniel and Charity to go ahead without her.

Fact was, she hadn't talked much to Ivan since she'd broken things off with him so abruptly. Just that once when she'd blurted that business about his green card expiring. That hadn't been right, at least not the way she'd said it.

Recalibrating was tricky. It seemed best to just keep things light as they traversed the blocks to her brownstone. Stick to safe subjects. As usual, Ivan went along with it, matching his stride to hers. By the time they reached her block, they'd chatted about every single thing Hope could think of, everything except the I.N.S. Agency crowding the walk between them.

Finally, they were there.

Hope lingered at the bottom of the steps that led up to her apartment building's door. As fond as she was of Ivan, it would be so easy to just fall back into her old rhythms with him. *Hold the line, now,* she reminded herself.

Ivan leaned against the iron rail beside her. "You sure I cannot come up?"

Something melted inside her. He wasn't going to make this easy. She forced herself to woman up. "Sorry. Full house at the moment."

Ivan shrugged congenially. "So, we hang out. Play an American board game. Like friends do."

Avoiding the conversation seemed fruitless. But it didn't make it any easier for her to look him in the eye. "This isn't fair to you, Ivan. I feel like I'm leading you on."

Ivan put his arms out to his sides, his palms exposed. "There is no false impression. You refused my proposal of marriage. Everything is completely understood."

She glanced up toward the sky. "Still..."

Ivan swung around to face her squarely. "Hope, listen to me. I have accepted that I will be deported in a month."

"Why?" Hope asked. "There's still time. Who knows? Maybe you could meet someone else."

Ivan shuffled his foot against the walk. "I suppose I could. But how fair would that be to see someone else, when all I would think of is you?"

"Ivan..." Hope had to turn away. It was just too hard to look at him. What, with those dark chocolate eyes.

Ivan softly brushed her arm, drawing her gaze back to him. "You do not have to feel what I feel, Hope. And please. I do not want you to feel bad that I feel it."

Hope dropped her head. "How can I not feel bad?"

Ivan gently raised her chin with his hand. "I do not. Why would I feel bad for feeling the best feeling I have ever felt?"

"Um...because I rejected you?"

An unexpected grin curled on his lips. "Silly woman. Do you know how alone I was in this city until I met you?"

Everything in Hope wanted to answer. Yes, she did understand. She completely got what it was like to feel desperately alone in the city. She knew the soul-level loneliness of having no one to call her own.

Absolutely.

But the words refused to come from her lips.

Ivan sighed. There was a wistful resignation about him that she couldn't help notice as he scanned down the street. "All my life, I dreamed of coming to this country. Sergei and Anton, they remember. I had this fantasy that I would build a family, become a great chef. Maybe that I would even become a success, make my name known."

Hope allowed herself to smile. "Yeah. I guess I did that last one, too."

"Sure," Ivan nodded. "Because, well, that is how dreams are. But here is my reality: there is no business, no family. No. I am not rich. I am not sought after, except by immigration. And what does it matter? In the end, it has not been about any of those things. I do not dream of anything anymore. Nothing but you."

There was something so disarming about the way Ivan spoke. It was the truth, she realized. He was being more honest with her than she'd even been with herself.

"Hope—all this time I have been here—when I think of it, the very best of it has been with you. No, you did not tell me much about your past. But who you have been to me here, in the present, that I will never forget. When I go back, that is all I want to take with me. That I have a friend in America." He paused. "Just a friend, that is all. Someone who will maybe remember me a little bit. Someone who cares that I was once here." Ivan searched her brimming eyes. "I will not ask any more of you, Hope, but can you do that?"

Hope could only nod. It was impossible not to remember how much she adored him, to recall why she'd taken to him so readily in the first place. He was cut off from his homeland, just like she was. The difference was that he would be compelled to return soon. He'd be forced to leave the life he always wanted to live. Maybe it would be just as well if he did. Maybe he was meant to go back. Maybe she was, too.

Hope nodded. She returned Ivan's gaze. He hadn't asked much. Only friendship. It seemed the very least she could do for him. "Yeah, Ivan," she promised. "I can be your friend back here. I can do that."

twelve

Charity sat across from Daniel, fashioning a tiny white apron for a handmade doll. He had been so quiet that evening. He'd hardly said a thing since she'd whispered to him about what happened with Leanne.

She was still in there. Not a sound had come from that room since Charity had left. Maybe he was afraid Leanne would overhear them through her door. Maybe he was just tired. The sofa was comfortable enough for sitting, but sleeping there might well be catching up with him.

She looked up from the doll. Warmly, Daniel returned her smile, then went back to painting his carving. His eyes looked so soft, his lids heavy. He's just weary. Surely, that must be it. She should focus on her work and allow him to concentrate on his. They didn't need to talk all the time. In this noisy city, silence was a gift they could give to each other.

The doll she was making was coming together nicely. A black bonnet already surrounded its blank muslin face. There had been plenty of leftover violet fabric from her own dress to make one for the doll. All in all, it looked just like the one Mamm had made for her when she was a little girl. Many layers of muslin had been sewn over that old doll, preserving it over the years she'd played with it. The last layer she had patched on herself, before putting the doll away for safekeeping. One day, that old doll would be a gift, should Gott bless her with a daughter.

The doll she was making now—that would be for Daniel's sister, Abby, this Christmas. Hopefully, it would make Abby smile. At sixteen, though Abby had blossomed physically, she still had the mind of a child. So sweet and trusting. No wonder Daniel was so protective of her, especially now that she'd come of age to go to Sunday singings. That must have been why he'd always gone, ever since Abby had started to go.

What a good brother Daniel was. And what a good husband he would be. At least that seemed to be where things between them were headed. After all, he had told her that he loved her. Still, he hadn't said much since. So much had happened since then, though.

Was something she had said or done bothering him? He hadn't been unpleasant in any way. Not at all. That wasn't his nature. He just sat, diligently painting that horse and buggy toy he'd carved for his brother.

Charity snipped a new length of white thread. "With two brothers, I never made dolls. You think Abby will like this?"

Daniel glanced up at her. "My sister would love whatever you give her."

"You don't think she's too old for dolls? Maybe I should make her a new bonnet instead."

A fond understanding crossed his face as he dabbed his brush into the paint. "Knowing Abby, I think she'd prefer the doll."

The lull in conversation that followed ate at Charity. Why it was that things suddenly seemed so awkward between them, she couldn't be sure. Maybe she should just let it go. Everything was probably fine. Still, the knot in her stomach refused to release its grip. "Has something changed?"

Daniel looked up. "How do you mean?"

Charity searched for words. There was no turning back now. "I'm not really sure. You seem somehow...displeased with me."

His brow knitted. "Do I?"

Charity put the doll down and moved to Daniel's side on the sofa. She lowered her voice. "Is it because I kissed you?"

"No, not at all. Believe me."

"Is it because I gave the money I made to Leanne?"

"No. Of course, not."

Charity sat back, still unsettled in her spirit. "Then, it is something."

Daniel seemed to mull it over briefly before he turned his attention back to her. "You did well. Singing."

"Is it because I sang in harmony? Or with the piano?"

"No, it's... You did seem to enjoy it."

Charity studied him intently. "Does that give you some concern?"

Another moment or two passed before Daniel responded. "I suppose. That you would come to like it too well yet."

"Daniel, I was helping Aunt Hope. It was the only way. She needs her job."

"Not if she comes back with us."

Charity let out a sigh. He was right. "No. I guess not, but..." Why was she so conflicted? Life with the English hadn't been at all what she'd imagined it would be. It was not void of faith or the simple joys she relished in Amish life. There were just different joys to be discovered. Suddenly, it dawned on her. She was, indeed, feeling the pull of the English world. Dat had told her to expect it, but in fairness, it didn't seem like such a bad thing.

She studied Daniel. "You don't like it here much, do you now?"

Daniel raised a brow. "It doesn't matter so much if I like it or not. This isn't our life."

"It's Aunt Hope's life, though. And she's a part of me."

"She hasn't been. Not anymore. Not since she chose to leave us."

Nothing in Charity wanted to challenge Daniel. Yet, honesty compelled her. Somehow she should find the strength she needed. Before she could hold them back, tears overtook her. "I know what you're saying, Daniel, but at the same time... I guess I don't know anymore. Not for sure."

Daniel set aside the paints and lovingly turned to her. "What? Tell me. What do you not know? There's nothing that you can't share with me."

As she searched his eyes, what she saw was compassion. She really could tell him anything, even the hard truth that was troubling her. "If she won't come back with us, I don't know if I could keep shutting her out, just because she lives in the world. I'm sorry, Daniel, but is that so wrong? Aunt Hope trusts the same Gott that we do. She lives our faith. She is kind and giving."

"And she has abandoned the vows of her baptism, vows she made to Gott," Daniel whispered. He glanced toward Leanne's door. "She has broken the heart of her father. She has deserted her family, her friends. You have to see it in that light."

Charity tried to absorb it, but his words wrestled with the conviction growing inside her. "She would have visited if she'd felt welcome to come and go. I'm sure. With the changes, there are others in our district that loved ones who were once shunned visit on occasion. The bishop allowed it. And they at least exchange letters from time to time."

Gently, he covered her hand with his. "Charity, people look up to your father. They respect mine, too. Yes, there are those few at home who are starting to make these concessions, but by far, they're in the minority. It's just the Beacheys. That isn't the example our fathers have set, or that they've asked us to honor."

Charity nodded, understanding. Still, it was hard to fathom what good cutting her Aunt Hope off completely had done. "Dat says she has written to us every Christmas. We're the ones who don't respond. Can you imagine how she would feel after this?"

Daniel laced his fingers into hers. "I've thought about this, too, Charity. And even if we did respond, if we let her visit, the problem is that she'd never come back to stay. Then, more and more, others would join the few who want to do it now. You know they would. In and out, English and Amish, till the life we know would be lost forever."

Charity absorbed it thoughtfully. He had an undeniable point, and he had made it with such patience. It made her admire him all the more. It told her she was safe with him. That she could reveal the deepest secrets of her heart.

"Yes, Daniel. I know what you're saying, but... Between us, does it ever set you to wonder? Do you ever question these things at all?"

Daniel sat quietly. "No."

"Honestly."

"It seems you do." From the look he returned, Charity could tell that Daniel was more than concerned. He broke her gaze sadly.

All at once, Leanne burst through her door, shattering their silence. Daniel released her hand.

Leanne marched straight to the coffee table where Daniel had been working and slapped Charity's money down. "There! Count it if you want." The pile of coins she'd pilfered came next, in fitful handfuls, fished from her pockets. "That's all of it."

Charity raised her hands. "Leanne, stop. You don't have to do this. Just put the quarters back in the tip jar along with what I gave you. This whole thing can stay between us."

"I'm a runaway," Leanne spat. "I'm giving up my own baby to who knows who. I totally ripped Hope off. And, what, you're not gonna turn me in?"

Daniel shook his head. "Turning you in... That's... It's just not our way."

The front door opened. Aunt Hope eased into the room. Charity's gaze darted to Aunt Hope as Leanne wagged an insistent finger at Daniel. "No, your way is... See, you don't have to say a word. Uh-uh. You just sit there all glowy and wonderful, showing up what a complete mound of mess I am!"

Hope strode to Charity's side. "Leanne!"

Charity rose. "It's all right."

Hotly, Leanne blurted. "No, it ain't all right!" She turned to Aunt Hope. "I stole your tips, then she gave me what I needed to pay you back. So, go ahead. Here's your chance. Go on, boot me!"

A bewildered look on her face, Aunt Hope faced Leanne. "Leanne... I'm not going to put you out of here."

Leanne flashed from Charity and Daniel. She whirled back to Aunt Hope. "None of y'all get it, do you? I'm a bad person. I royally destroy everything I manage to touch. I got nobody! I been crampin' somethin' awful all day and got nothin' to go to a doctor—"

Aunt Hope's eyes widened. "You're in labor?"

"No, course not. Can't be," Leanne winced. "I still got a month to go before—"

Charity exchanged a concerned glance with Aunt Hope. "How long between the cramps?"

"What difference does it make?" Leanne squeezed at her middle.

Taking Leanne by the arms, Aunt Hope focused straight into her eyes. "Leanne, stop. I want you to answer me, just one question. How long between the cramps?"

Leanne shifted restlessly. "I don't know. It's not like I'm counting. Couple-three minutes maybe."

It hadn't been so very long since Charity had assisted in the birth of Daniel's cousin, Lydia's baby. Lydia had borne up very bravely. She'd barely whimpered, despite the length of her labor. Still, pushing had to have been so very painful. Even just watching how traumatic that birth had been had left Charity lightheaded. Thank Gott for the midwife, though. Thank Gott that, step-by-step, that midwife had talked her through the entire process with Lydia. Charity laid a hand on her heart.

Please Gott, help me remember.

Leanne lay on the futon, buckled over with a contraction. Charity checked beneath her skirt, just as the mid-wife had shown her with Lydia. Charity caught her breath. The baby was already crowning.

Aunt Hope burst in with her keys. "We should get her to the hospital."

Charity shook her head. "There's no time. She's too close."

Leanne writhed. "I'm having this baby now?"

Gently, Charity lowered Leanne's skirt. "Soon. Just breathe."

Panic raced across Leanne's face. She searched Charity's eyes. "You know how to do this?"

"So I do," Charity nodded, as much for Aunt Hope's sake as for Leanne's. "Aunt Hope, would you please ask Daniel to boil some water? Use it to sterilize a sharp knife and a needle from my sewing kit. There's some thread in there, too."

Leanne trembled. "You have to cut me?"

"Just the cord, let's pray."

Aunt Hope started for the door. "I'm calling an ambulance. I'm not going to let her—"

"I told you no ambulances!" Leanne screamed. "I can't pay for no hospital!"

Calmly, Charity intervened. "Aunt Hope, it's almost time. They couldn't get here anyway. The baby is in a good position. We'll be all right. Just tell Daniel what I need."

Horrorstruck, Leanne erupted. "No! I can't do this. It hurts!"

Charity leaned forward, her gaze quite intent. "Leanne, I want you to look at me." Try as she might, she could not catch the thrashing girl's eyes. "No, right here, Leanne. Breathe with me."

Methodically, Charity demonstrated. Finally. Leanne started to match Charity's breaths. Charity whispered to Aunt Hope. "Can you get started with those things we need?" A look of grave concern weighed heavily on Aunt Hope's face, but she left compliantly.

Charity turned back to Leanne, her words measured and sure. "When I say so, I'm going to need you to push. Until then, just keep up your breathing, okay?"

"Okay," Leanne whimpered.

By the time Hope reached the kitchen, Daniel was already running water into a stainless steel pot. Instinctively, she reached into a cabinet for a tempered glass pitcher. "Even with a gas stove, the microwave's faster. But we can't use metal in there."

Daniel hesitated. Just as she expected, he was avoiding the microwave. Out of respect for them, she'd avoided it, too, up until then, but he would just have to understand.

Determined, Hope edged Daniel out of her way. She swiveled the faucet to her side, and started to fill the pitcher. "Look, Daniel, boiling water is boiling water. God created electricity anyway. What do you think lightning is? The microwave just harnesses that power. You know what? If it's sin, I'll take it on me. Just let me do it."

Raising his hands, Daniel stepped back.

Hope felt horrible immediately. She, of all people, should be more compassionate about where he was coming from. Still, the memories that this moment evoked flooded back in excruciatingly vivid detail. She had boiled water then. She had coached Grace with her breathing as Aaron and Isaac had entered this world, one right after the other. She had held Grace's sweet hand until all the warmth drained out of it and the spark of life had left her eyes. There was an absence about that look that she would never forget.

Hope checked the slowly filling pitcher. Get it together, she coached herself. Let him help how he can. "I'm sorry. I'm just... There's a hand sharpener in the drawer to put a fresh edge on that knife. Could you give me a hand with that?"

Daniel opened Hope's utensil drawer and started to root around. "She'll be all right."

Hope shut the spigot off. "With all respect—and I'm really trying to give you that, Daniel—you don't know she'll be all right. You can't know that. Only the good Lord does." She placed the water pitcher into the microwave and started it.

Daniel located the sharpener. "Charity has helped birth a baby before. My cousin, Lydia's."

"So had I," Hope recalled. "I also watched her mother die, exactly this way." She hurried into the living room and grabbed Charity's sewing kit.

Daniel began to draw the knife's blade against the sharpener. "Has no woman ever died giving birth in a hospital?"

Returning, Hope pulled the lid off Charity's basket. "I'm sure some do. That's not the point."

Daniel sharpened the knife expertly. His words were calm, yet penetrating, all at the same time. "And did you abandon the city because of it?"

"Daniel..."

"No, you didn't. Because, as sad as it is, people die. It happens in hospitals, and it happens at home. It's a part of life."

Hot tears burned Hope's eyes. "Grace did not have to die."

Daniel took it in contemplatively. "We all have to die sometime."

Wiping her face, Hope pulled a needle from Charity's kit. Long buried anger burned in her throat. "She was the best friend I had in this world, and she did not have to leave us. Not then."

They turned at the sound of a newborn's cry.

Hope threw open the door to Leanne's room, just in time to see Charity rise with the fretful infant.

Leanne reached out, soaked with emotion. Hope closed the door and slumped against it. She pressed a hand to her heaving chest. So far, they were okay.

Charity beamed at Leanne. "You have a son."

Leanne laughed through her tears. "A boy? Oh, look... Can I?"

Carefully, Charity extended the baby to Leanne. "You can hold him. There."

Hope watched wordlessly as Leanne gazed in amazement at her son. From all appearances, she would be all right.

"Look Hope. He's so little. And, yikes. So gunky. Is that okay?"

A smile curled across Charity's lips. "He's fine. We'll get some salt and clean him up."

Leanne drew her infant close. "Shhh, Darlin'. It's all right. I'm here. I'm here."

Serenely, Charity looked up. Hope leaned her head back against the doorjamb, relieved beyond words. No matter the circumstances, a new life had safely come into this world. It seemed a sacred privilege to be part of it.

When Hope emerged from Leanne's room, she found Daniel waiting quietly. He was far from an expectant father, she thought, but he still had that familiar look of concern on his face as he stood there. It reminded her of Nathan's expression when the twins had come, so many years ago. What a bittersweet responsibility it had been to break the news to her brother that, while he was the father of two infant sons, his dear wife had died in the process.

Hope did her best to shake off the past as she moved to Daniel's side. "They're fine. Charity did a good job."

Daniel nodded.

As hard as she tried to prevent it, a tear slipped down Hope's cheek.

Tenderly, Daniel brushed her shoulder, then sat down on the couch. "It was a long time ago. But I am sorry for your loss."

Hope wiped her face. "It was Charity's loss, too. Her mother."

Daniel's eyes were filled with understanding. "Yes. And your best friend."

Hope sat beside him, deep in thought. "Did you know Charity's mother?"

"I was only seven, so not much, but my parents knew her," Daniel replied. "They said she was a good woman. We all stood with her at her burial. It rained that day. Seems like an odd memory."

So, he had been there. Daniel never intended to hurt her, but even the mere mention of Grace's burial plagued her. At the time, she'd been far too overwhelmed with grief and anger to even think about attending. Instead, she'd found herself leaving them all. She'd quietly slipped away from everything and everyone she had ever held dear. Even when she'd told Nathan she'd just be revisiting her Rumspringa, she'd known it was much more.

Hope exchanged a solemn look with Daniel. "I wish I had done things differently. I guess I just couldn't face saying goodbye to her, and acting like it was okay. I didn't think I'd miss my family as much as I did. Still do." She shook her head and shrugged her shoulders. "And now my own mother is gone. Can't change that."

Daniel shook his head softly. "No. But you can change your future. You can come home now."

Hope breathed in deeply. She really should consider it. Seriously, this time. For a moment, she allowed herself to think it: *I'm going home.* But as soon as those words crossed her mind, the realities she knew she'd have to face came tumbling over top of them.

She turned to regard him. "Tell me something, Daniel. Honestly, I'm not trying to be adversarial. I just really need to know. Not what you think I'd like to hear, but the truth."

Holding her gaze, Daniel nodded. "All right."

Hope paused. This was sensitive territory. "I know your community is more conservative than some about childbirth, and even then, a few of the younger generation differ about medical care. I also understand the financial challenges since the Amish have no health insurance. So, I just have to ask..." She took a measured breath. "If it were Charity's life on the line—if she were the one you could save by going to a hospital to give birth—would you take her to one?"

A sober expression formed on Daniel's face. "I believe what they teach us," he started, "that it is not about the death we fear, so much as the life we choose to live." Daniel paused. "It would be agony, yes. It would be the greatest test of my faith." He stopped again, his eyes glistening. "Honestly, I don't know. But I hope I would choose to have our children born in the comfort of our home, and trust Gott to do what's best."

Hope nodded, taking it in. A part of her wanted to rail at him. Why would he stand so stalwartly by such outdated medical practices, even at the risk of a life so precious as Charity's? But the other part of her admired his conviction, and the love he so clearly had for her niece.

Daniel was every bit like Nathan, Hope realized. He was a good, devout man who would love Charity every single day that she had breath. But the thought that Charity's life could be unnecessarily cut short, that weighed as heavy on her heart as the decision she had to make. Either way, she realized, she would be grieving again. One way or another, she would have to say goodbye.

thirteen

As the days added up to nearly three weeks in the city, Charity found herself falling into a rhythm. Night after night, she'd record what had happened in a journal. She had started it for Bethany, but she realized that she wanted it just as much as a keepsake for herself.

These weeks, she'd never forget.

She wrote about getting to know Aunt Hope, and how they'd whisper late into the night about every little thing. She recounted what fun ice-skating was and how fascinating the hospital had been, despite Aunt Hope's still-mending wrist. Entries on what she experienced in the English church weren't so very Amish, but Bethany would understand.

There had the rosy color in Leanne's baby's cheeks to document, and what it was like to cook with gas instead of their wood-burning stove. It made her blush all over again to write how she'd been wearing that English uniform and caroling into a microphone for the sake of Aunt Hope's job.

When it came to the details with Daniel—well, they seemed almost too precious to confide via pen and paper. Her heart swelled just to think of the things he'd said to her, and the miracle of what was growing between them. These were secrets she would only write on her heart. She would save them to share with Bethany face to face.

One thing was for certain. This had been a trip she would always remember. How quickly the time had passed. Though so different from what she had known, life in the city had become familiar, and not so frightening as it once had been. It was easy to see how the English world could grow on a person, and how quickly the use of technology could become an everyday practice. She had never considered it a hardship to do without such things. Then again, until now, she hadn't had much basis for comparison.

Despite the differences, some of the essentials seemed exactly the same. When morning came, she rose, said a prayer of thanks, and began to make breakfast for everyone, just like she always did at home. Work at the Café Troubadour was brisk, but no more so than her regular chores. What she enjoyed, she realized, were not the glittery trappings of modern life. It was the people she lived and worked with there that were finding a place in her heart. Customers were beginning to ask for her, and call her by name. Even Goldie. Now, Christmas week was upon them. It was hard to believe that, in just a matter of days, they'd be boarding the train once again.

Charity placed napkins and utensils around a booth at the café. There was something satisfying about resetting a table that Daniel had freshly bussed. She loved exchanging those affectionate looks with him in passing. They communicated so much. Daniel had become a treasured part of her days, and she relished every moment with him.

Frank and Myrna were growing on her, too. Also, Shep was a sheer delight. What a special man he was, always a smile and a kind word, and never a complaint. She wondered just how it was that he'd learned all the music he seemed to know, how despite his blindness, his fingers found their way so effortlessly across the piano keys. *It must be a gift*, she decided.

Charity watched as Shep accompanied Aunt Hope, his faithful guide dog lounging at his feet. Shep softly swayed on his bench as Hope sang to the café's patrons. It wasn't a carol Charity had heard before, but the melody was liltingly pleasant. Most of all, it was the lyrics that caught her attention. It was something about a vow to be home for Christmas, a promise to be counted on for certain, whether in reality or in a dream.

There was such a faraway look in her Aunt Hope's eyes as she sang that particular song. There was a bittersweet longing, the likes of which Charity hadn't yet seen. She could only hope her aunt meant those words she was singing, and that something in that song was helping her to make peace with the idea of finally returning home.

Something about Ivan was growing on Charity. It was hard to put her finger on exactly what it was. Maybe it was pity over his childhood. Maybe it was the way he kept going to Aunt Hope's church and remained such a jubilant part of the choir each Sunday, even after she had broken things off with him. It could have been the shoeblack stains on his fingertips, how it told of much hard work. Then again, it was probably the way he'd wait outside the Troubadour each night at closing time, wanting to see Aunt Hope safely back to her apartment.

Manhattan was pretty at night. Charity had to admit it. Though a crush of sights and sounds, it seemed more tranquil somehow, once night fell. There was something blissful about strolling back toward Hope's apartment—Daniel at her side, and

Ivan at Aunt Hope's—the city sparkling with a million lights. It begged her to drink in the moment.

Along the way, they came upon a makeshift forest of fresh cut Christmas trees. Aunt Hope paused. She took an evergreen bough in her hand, leaned close, and drank in the aroma.

The tree vendor ambled over. "We got your blue spruce, your balsam fir, scotch pine... Take your pick."

Aunt Hope turned. "Pure heaven, aren't they?"

Charity took a whiff. "By now, Dat has brought cut greens inside from the woods. I suppose the twins helped him to arrange them this year. I'll bring the holly in from the yard on Christmas Eve so the berries will be fresh yet."

Daniel took in the scent. "Getting close now."

"Who lights the Christmas candle these days?" Aunt Hope asked.

"I do. Or I should say, I have." It touched Charity to realize that Aunt Hope remembered their family tradition after so many years. "It'll pass to the twins next, although I don't know which one will do it. Aaron thinks it should come to him since he was born first. But Dat said it's the candle or carving the turkey. Of course, Aaron doesn't want to give that up either, but one or the other will go to Isaac."

Aunt Hope smiled wryly. "I'd definitely hold out for the candle."

The tree vendor straightened a stately tree. "Just so you know... These beauties are all twenty-five percent off since it's Christmas week."

Ivan's eyes lit up as he turned to Hope. "Would you like one? I would be glad to carry it for you."

Aunt Hope looked over the tree longingly. Finally, she shook her head with a glance toward Charity and Daniel. "No. Christmas trees...see, Ivan, the Amish, they don't really have them in their homes. Their decorations are much simpler, so—"

"A wreath, then," Ivan went on, "for your door. I insist."

Charity glanced between them. "A wreath is just a small gathering of greenery. Could be a good compromise." Daniel nodded in agreement.

Aunt Hope pressed her lips. "Well..."

Ivan took Aunt Hope by her good arm. "Let me do this. Come over here, and we will pick out a nice one." She looked back only briefly as Ivan led her away, toward the display of wreaths.

As they waited, Charity wandered the lot with Daniel. Soon, they were surrounded by evergreens. In a way, it was as if the city had disappeared. Charity took in the aroma of balsam. "Not quite like the woods at home, but wonderful still."

Daniel took Charity in his arms. He drew her close. "I think I like having more trees around me than people," he confided.

Playfully Charity stepped away. "Should I leave you, then?" She didn't get far before Daniel pulled her back into a kiss. In the chill of the night air, his warm lips were especially inviting. It was as if he were communicating with her, freely expressing just how much she meant to him. After a moment, Charity broke away from him. She couldn't help blushing. "Daniel, they'll come back."

"And if they do...?" Daniel drew Charity into yet another kiss.

"They'll see," Charity whispered, her lips barely leaving his.

"Yes," Daniel acknowledged, not seeming to mind at all. "They'll see that I love you more with each passing day. That I want you to be my wife."

Charity gazed at Daniel, stunned. How far they'd come in such a very short time. There had never been anyone else for her, not in her whole life growing up as his friend and neighbor. But there was so much they hadn't talked about yet, so much they hadn't said before this trip.

Everything in her wanted to accept his proposal immediately. She longed to talk all about being published at church, to commit to a life with him amongst the Amish. But how could she not feel torn by the unresolved situation with Aunt Hope? Still, there was no mistaking it. The pull of his heart on hers was undeniable. Where were the words?

Taking her hands in his, Daniel looked full into Charity's face. He never wavered, almost as if he knew what she was thinking. "I realize that you have family obligations," he began, "and that there are many things you need to put to mind yet. I promise, I will do my best not to press you. But when we get back, know this is my intent."

Hope unlocked her apartment, then stood aside for Charity to enter. Ivan lingered at the door with Daniel, examining the burnished brass knocker. No doubt, he had spotted it as a place to attach the wreath. *Men love a project*, Hope recalled. They would waste no time embarking upon this one.

Inside, Leanne wrapped a soft cotton blanket around her freshly changed baby. Hope was surprised to see a box of diapers and an array of infant products on the coffee table. Frankly, Hope hadn't expected to see the baby still there at all. Hadn't Leanne's appointment with the adoption agency been that afternoon?

As much as she was tempted to ask about it, Hope reminded herself not to push. Just like Hope, Leanne was at a crossroads. She faced a decision that would define the rest of her life, and she needed to make it herself.

Ivan released the knocker with a clack. "Daniel, do you have some twine?"

Charity removed her bonnet. "You could use some of my thread. I have a heavy gauge spool that would work." With that, Charity was off to fetch her sewing basket.

Leanne bounced the baby in her arms, an eye toward Ivan at the door. "Well, good. You got a wreath to hang. It's about time it started lookin' like Christmas around here."

As she took off her coat, Hope wandered over toward Leanne and the baby. "Leanne, I thought... What's all this?"

Leanne used a small cloth to blot spit-up from the baby's face. "I know. I know. I told you I was givin' him up this morning. I even went by the adoption place. But he's so little... I decided to keep him a few more days. Let him get stronger, you know?"

It was a delicate subject Hope knew she needed to broach. Better not to loom over Leanne for this. She took a seat beside her on the sofa. The baby's eyes fluttered to a close as he drifted off to sleep. So tiny and sweet. No wonder Leanne had found it difficult to part with him. Surely, bonds were already growing as she'd been nursing him at her breast.

Hope loved everything about babies, from the scent of an infant's head to its impossibly tiny fingers and toes with those paper-thin nails. How long had she dreamed of having a child of her own one day? The nagging questions for her were always *where* and *with whom*. That was part of what had made the decision to reject Ivan's proposal so difficult. Her own procrastination gnawing at her, she turned to Leanne. "You know it won't be any easier to give him up down the road."

Leanne stroked her baby's soft tuft of dark hair. "Tell me somethin' I don't know. Truth is, I hate to give him up at all. I just don't see how I can work and take care of him. Poor little guy don't even have a name yet. How pitiful is that?"

Hope thought about how much easier it was to see answers for Leanne than it was for herself. Perhaps it was her maternal instincts kicking in, or maybe the fact that Leanne wasn't much more than a child herself. "There is a way, you know."

Leanne shook her head. "Okay. If I couldn't face my parents when I got pregnant, how am I supposed to tell them I have a baby?"

Regret washed over Hope. It was one of those familiar waves that would ebb in time, then come back to crash on her all over again. She had waited too long to go back to her own parents, till her mother had passed. It all seemed so final, so unchangeable for her, but maybe, just maybe, it wasn't too late for Leanne.

"Leanne, your mom and dad... Are they good people?"

Leanne's eyes misted at the thought. "They're over-the-top fantabulous people. They're everything I'm not."

Hope empathized. She'd thought that about her own parents, more times that she could count. Her mother had been an extraordinary woman of faith. She was reflexively forgiving and kind, with an underlying strength that seemed far beyond her petite frame. She'd had a gift for encouragement, something Hope tried to emulate.

Gently, Hope stroked the baby's head. "You carried this baby when a lot of girls wouldn't have. I think that's pretty great."

Leanne brightened noticeably. She looked almost dumfounded. "Really?"

Just then, Charity returned with the heavy thread and scissors. She passed on her way toward the door.

Hope put a comforting hand on Leanne's shoulder. "Yeah. I do. And I can't help but think that your mom would want to meet her grandson."

Panic chased across Leanne's expression. "Oh, I don't know."

"He's their family, too," Hope assured. "And that bond, it's bigger than all the mess-ups and all the miles you could ever put between you."

Leanne wrinkled her nose. "I thought about callin' plenty of times. It's just... I can't seem to pick up the phone."

Hope glanced over to the door where Charity and Daniel helped Ivan with the wreath. She looked back at Leanne, her voice steadied by personal conviction. "They'll take you back, Leanne. I know it. Just like my family would take me."

Alone in her bedroom, Hope slid open her bottom dresser drawer. She felt beyond her cardigans and socks, deep into the back, and pulled out a small bundle, wrapped in tissue. How long it had been stowed away, Hope wasn't sure. She only knew it felt like reaching back in time, to a far away place, to an era that seemed far too distant to recapture.

Almost reverently, Hope unfolded the tissue. Inside was her old prayer covering, the white kapp she'd worn so long ago, after being baptized at seventeen. Bittersweet memories flooded. Even then, she'd known her motives hadn't been entirely pure. She had given her life to the Lord to be sure, but there was something else she'd been given over to that day, something she'd never told anyone, no one except Charity's mother, Grace.

It was a secret Grace had taken to her grave.

That long-regretted truth, that was the reason Hope had committed to the Amish life as hastily as she did. Without question, her profession of faith had been sincere, but when she was completely honest with herself, she had made it at the time that she did in the hopes of impressing that young man: Joseph Glick.

A few years older than she, Joseph had already been a member of the church. He'd been following in the footsteps of his father, their bishop. Joseph was so handsome, so committed to the Amish way of life. He'd been very friendly with her at a number of the singings, while undecided about whom he might pursue as a wife. Constance had been closer to his age, but in Hope's mind, she'd seen herself as being every bit as mature.

So, she had donned this very white kapp.

She had rushed to take her vows.

And she had secretly prayed that Joseph would take notice of her as the woman she was becoming.

What a fraud she was. She hadn't deserved him at all. It hadn't been long afterward that Joseph began to call on Constance. When he did, it had pierced Hope beyond what she'd felt she could survive. Only Grace had known how she had wept for him. Only Grace had realized how deeply she had repented, how she'd tarnished the purity of her baptism with unrequited longing for a man.

Funny, how quickly her feelings for Joseph had faded. She had long gotten over him. That pain had paled as the girlhood crush that it was. But the gaping wound that had remained open for seventeen years, that had been the devastating loss of Grace, so very soon to follow.

It hadn't seemed possible that Grace could have been so alive, so brimming with joy over the birth of twin sons, then gone forever in the very next moment. Modern medicine could have saved her, yet she'd held Grace's hand and watched her die, before Grace ever even cradled her own sons.

That had done it for her. That was when she'd packed what little she owned and gathered all the money she had to her name. It had been far too difficult to face her parents. It was cowardly, but she had made her excuses to them in a letter.

Only Nathan had seen her slip out. In his brotherly way, he had done his best to calm her. She could still hear his voice. How he tried to persuade her to give herself time to grieve along with the rest of them. But she had shut his pleas out, far too distraught to listen.

That was when she had boarded the train in town. She'd made her way to New York City. That week, she had taken off her kapp for the last time, and sheared her long hair for the first. She had sold her locks to a place that made wigs for cancer patients. To think it would cover another woman's head helped her get over her guilt in cutting it. Shame had lingered, but it ebbed over time.

All those Plain dresses she'd brought to the city... What had she been thinking? How out of place she'd felt wearing them from the very first day. She'd picked up some English clothes, gotten her G.E.D. and gone straight to work amongst them, without a word of who she was, or what her upbringing had been. Day after day, she'd distanced herself from the person she had been. She'd drifted farther and farther from the family she adored.

Lost in thought, Hope barely noticed when Charity entered.

Charity saw the kapp in her hands immediately. "You still have yours."

A nostalgic smile crept across Hope's lips. "Just the one. I figured I'd need it if I ever went back." Hope turned toward the mirror. For the first time in many years, she eased the covering over her shoulder-length tresses. Silently, Charity stepped up behind her as she studied her image.

Hope drew the kapp's ribbons forward over her shoulders. "Wow. Weighty little thing."

Charity nodded. "Means a lot."

"Brings a lot back," Hope confessed.

There were times it seemed that Charity could see right through her, just the way Grace always had.

"Good things?" Charity asked.

Hope could only sigh. "Almost entirely. Your mamm made this kapp, you know. She sewed it up special, for my baptism."

Charity ran her fingers along the laces of her own kapp. "She made this one, too. Dat gave it to me when I turned eighteen. It's the last of the kapps she made. I never want to part with it."

Hope wrapped an arm around Charity. "You're so much like her, you know? Grace always loved what was meaningful much more than what was new. She had this exquisite stillness about her."

Charity nodded softly, "Dat says the very same thing. So he does."

The memory of Grace's serene face filled Hope's mind. "Things would happen and she was just...quiet. Purposed. Grounded. Exactly the way you were, delivering that baby."

Hope took a seat on the bed. "I was the one with the restless streak. I always blame my leaving on her death, or a tiny bit on Joseph rejecting me, but... Maybe there was just something in me that wanted to venture out, see the world, and I found some sort of validation in those other reasons. That's always been my story, but... Maybe I would have left anyway. I don't know."

Soberly, Hope removed the kapp. As she held it in her hands, it dawned on her. She'd finally come to a decision. She was sure. Now, all that was left was to tell Charity, and to hope that somehow she'd understand. "You know, I realized this morning that I've gone almost as many years without one of these kapps on as I had with one."

A knowing expression registered on Charity's face. "You've made a decision."

"Yeah. I think I just have." Hope raised her eyes as they began to moisten. "And I've got to say, it just about rips my heart in two."

Hope took Charity's hands in hers. "I love you so much, Charity. You were too young to remember, but from the day you were born, you—it's like you responded to me, and everything in me responded to you."

"Like music," Charity smiled. "Blending. Like when you sing with me. That's how we are."

"Yes," Hope answered. "Like music. See? There you go again. You resonate with everything in me. Nothing manufactured, nothing at all planned, it's just...who you are. You're my heart."

Despite Hope's efforts to hold back, tears began to fall. "If you knew how many times I've cried and I've prayed that somehow I could be with all of you again and... Now, here you are, this incredible gift. Still loving me, still wanting me in your life, just as much as I want you."

"Then, come," Charity pleaded. "Please come."

Though the words formed in her mind, Hope could hardly bring herself to speak them. It wouldn't be right to lead Charity on a moment longer. She loved her too much for that.

"Charity, I wish I could go home with you. I do. But I really have thought about it, and I realize that I... I want a family of my own. There's still time left for me to have children—which for me pretty much requires a husband—and face it. Amish marry young. The community is so small. I'm into my mid thirties and I'm guessing there's probably not a single man left even close to my age. Not that I'd consider."

Charity sat quietly. "No one comes to mind."

"And it's not like there's an influx."

"Not much." Charity sighed. "Any chance that Ivan would come?"

Hope set her kapp aside. It wasn't as though she hadn't considered it. In many ways, Ivan had found his way into her heart. "Ivan would do anything for me. But I would never ask this of him. I just couldn't." She hung her head, knowing she'd never even asked it of herself. "For Ivan to become Amish would mean giving up so much of what he came to this country to find. Freedom to choose where and how to live and work and worship—those are really big things for him. They are for me, too. Like they were for the Amish when they migrated here."

Respectfully, Hope set her kapp back into the tissue paper. "I mean, I won't pretend it's just his issue," she said. "The truth is: this is my home now. As much as I ache for all of you—my life, and my chance to have a family of my own, now that I've been gone so many years, it's in the English world."

Sadly, Charity took Hope's hand in hers. "Are you sure?"

Hope hesitated. The finality of the decision ached in her chest. "I'm so sorry, Honey. But, yes. I am."

As Hope started to wrap the tissue over her kapp, Charity gently reached out to stop her.

"Wait." Wistfully, Charity removed the kapp from her head. She took Hope's kapp from the tissue paper and placed hers there instead. Finally, Charity situated Hope's kapp over her bun. "This way," Charity assured, "you will always be with me."

Hope wrapped her arms around her niece. "And I will be with you." How could she ever say goodbye to one so dear as Charity had already become to her? All she knew was that her heart was breaking. And in the balm of their embrace, years of pent up sorrow finally found its way free.

fourteen

Alone in Hope's apartment, except for her infant son, Leanne didn't feel so alone anymore. She'd always wondered what in the world young mothers could possibly do to entertain themselves all day. What a surprise it was to find herself completely content to feed the little guy and change his diaper, even just to watch him sleep. She could tell him anything, and it actually kind of seemed like he was listening.

Absently, she chewed at a hangnail. How amazing was it that this wonder of a creature had come from her body? It was also a huge relief that he had been safely born, completely outside of a doctor's care. She checked the nub where Charity had tied off his navel. Looked like a major outie at this point. It had turned kind of a purplish black, just like Charity had said it would. He was doing just fine, she confirmed, head to toe.

He'd even latched on and taken to nursing, right off the bat. What a freakish feeling that had been at first. Really. It had hurt a little, but she was getting the hang of it. There was something that felt pretty good about being able to give her child what he needed.

He gurgled as she bounced him on her shoulder, lightly patting his back. Next came the little burp she'd learned to encourage.

"There you go. That's a good boy. You feel better now, don't you?" She pulled him off her shoulder to get a look. As she spoke, the infant peered intently into her eyes. "Yes, that's right. That's a very good boy."

The baby's head bobbled a bit, as if in response, still rapt at the sight of her face.

Leanne watched him in fascination. Never, in over eight months of carrying this child, had she expected what came over her in that moment.

He was hers, and she was his.

It would always be that way, no matter what.

She leaned her face over toward his. "Do you know who I am, Little Guy? Do you? Don't tell nobody, 'cause it's a secret, but I'm your Momma. That's right. That's who I am." She took his hand in hers.

With that, the infant wrapped his tiny fingers around hers. Whoa. Already, he was such a strong little dude. She tugged a bit, testing him, and yet he hung on tightly.

Leanne grinned. "Look at you! Look at how strong you are." Sleepily, his eyes drifted to a close. Already, his little face reminded her of his father. Reggie would never know what he'd missed. She sat, mesmerized, watching the rise and fall of his chest with each breath. She pressed her ear to his body. There was the quiet whoosh of his heartbeat. He was a miracle for sure, way beyond her imaginings.

A thought pierced the silence. What had she ever done to deserve a miracle? He was so small, so helpless. He was sleeping so sweetly, completely unaware of what a world class wreck she'd made of her life, much less the mess she stood to make of his, left to her own devices. She rubbed her forehead, defeated.

There was no way she could do this. Not by herself.

Her eyes fell on Hope's telephone. Once again, the things Hope had said about her mom and dad rang in her ears. As much as she hated like absolute crazy-fits to face it, Hope was right. This was her parents' first grandson. He was part of their family, too.

Just the thought of her mother's face made Leanne want to pick up the phone. By now, she was making her melt-in-your-mouth gingerbread cookies with sweet white piping and raisins for buttons. They made the whole house smell amazing.

Their home number flashed across her mind. With Christmas so close, thinking of her mom had become pretty much a round–the-clock thing. Her mom loved babies. That was for sure. And it was hard to imagine that she wouldn't go goo-gobs of gaga over this one, no matter how he'd come to be.

Leanne straightened up, her attention fixed on the phone. She ran over the things that she might say. How would she start? Would she be able to speak at all without bursting into an absolute blubberfest? She inhaled deeply. "Okay, try to do this... Okay."

Leanne reached for the phone. She picked up the receiver and stared at the buttons for the longest kind of time, unable to do anything more.

Guilt washed over her.

Fear wasn't far behind.

What would they think of her? What would everyone they knew say? Mouths would sure drop and tongues would waggle once the neighbors found out. That cranky woman who lived across the street would say she'd seen it all coming. This person would call that one. The kids would tease Jay-Jay at his school. A truckload of shame would be dumped on her poor mom and dad. They'd be the ones with the wayward daughter, the one who got herself into trouble with some boy who'd hardly spoken to her since the morning after.

Slowly, Leanne put the receiver back down. She'd gotten herself into this mess, and she would have to get herself out of it.

Hope couldn't help but smile, seeing Ivan just inside the Troubadour's entry. There he was, freshly groomed, wearing a suit of all things. Ivan didn't have much. He hadn't needed anything in the way of business attire for cooking school, or for his job shining shoes on the street.

As it had happened, this particular suit was what had brought the two of them together, way back in June. Clueless about the finer points of fashion, Ivan had spotted her browsing in the second hand store. He'd asked her opinion about a tie. Back then, he'd been very up front with her about why he was suit shopping. He wanted to look nice when he went to appeal for his U.S. citizenship. Now, clearly, he'd dressed to impress Frank, and had decided that this same suit was the way to do it. In the process, he'd impressed her, too.

Ivan wasn't a mover or a shaker by any stretch. He wasn't really known, except to her. But there was something about his heart that had always beat in time with hers, in ways she simply could not deny. What was it about him? In so many respects, they were different. But at the core of who they were, they were the same. They'd both come to the city with the dream of making a new life, of finding a sense of belonging. They'd both found refuge in this place, far from homelands they'd both fled.

As much as she knew that, Hope still wrestled with the pull of her past. He probably did, too. As fiercely as she'd missed those she held so dear, Ivan shared that same struggle. She realized, better than most, what it was like to face that great divide, that chasm that separated them from their people and tore their hearts in two.

Just as she had, Ivan had chosen to pursue a life of independence. It wasn't that they'd never looked back. It wasn't that they didn't love those they'd left behind. But they'd both succumbed to a longing for adventure, a calling outside of their upbringings, a need to at least try to carve out lives of their own.

The difference, for Ivan, was that his dream was coming to an end.

As handsome as he'd looked in that suit and as ardently as he'd pursued getting U.S. citizenship, for some reason it had been repeatedly denied. Each passing day brought him closer to a reality that he hadn't chosen. Yet, there he stood tall, at the entrance of The Café Troubadour, wanting to spend the last days of his dream washing dishes, if only to be near her.

From the way Frank eyed Ivan at the doorway through the kitchen's pass-through window, it was pretty clear that Ivan had succeeded in getting his attention. The least she could do was help. Hope dogged Frank's steps as he grabbed the order that Myrna clipped to the wheel.

Frank glanced at the order. "He's wearing a suit. Who wears a suit to apply for a dishwasher job?"

Hope shot an encouraging wave toward Ivan. "Look, I'm sure he's just trying to make a good impression. Come on, Frank. Ease up. Just give him a chance."

Myrna picked up a steaming plate of scrambled eggs. "Yeah, Frank. Give him a go."

Frank strode back to the griddle. "I thought he was shipping out."

Hope followed him. "Not for a couple of weeks, but Charity and Daniel are leaving in two days." She ladled a crock of chili and sprinkled some cheese on top. "Who knows how long Leanne will be out recouping. Ivan can fill in. Look, he's a good man. He's a very hard worker. He's also a fantastic cook. Did you know that? Come on. What's your hesitation?"

As soon as she'd said those words to Frank, they echoed within her own heart. Why was she hesitating with Ivan? Why hadn't she told him anything of what was growing inside her? What was holding her back, now that she'd finally made her decision to stay? It wasn't lack of affection for him. She knew that of a certainty. She adored Ivan. Just seeing him there still moved her in ways she could hardly explain, even to herself.

It had been different long ago with Joseph Glick. That had only been a girlhood crush. Sure, she'd been devastated at the time, but that had passed within a matter of months. Inside her heart, Hope breathed a prayer. *Is this love?* As soon as she asked, a question came back to her, seemingly in response.

How will you feel when he leaves?

Immediately, Hope was heartsick to her core. It was hard enough to face that Charity and Daniel would soon be going. She ached to think that Ivan be next, in just a few short weeks, when he would be deported.

Regret whirled around her mind. How could she have been so thoughtless to accuse Ivan of using her to get his green card the way she had? Sure, his proposal had been rushed, but she knew in her heart that it had been far from insincere.

From the very beginning, they'd had a real connection. It had meant so much to her that he'd shared her faith, and that he always sang with such gusto in the choir. He longed to set down roots and start a family, like she did. He was gentle and funny and sweet.

Soon, given the chance, Ivan could graduate from cooking school. He might get a good job as a chef, maybe even there, with Frank. Surely, he'd work hard to provide. He would make a wonderful father. What's more, she'd never detected the slightest hint of deceit in him, not in all the time that she'd known him. Why had she been so quick to push him away? Why had she made a liar of herself by denying how very much she knew that she loved him, too?

Charity strolled along the sidewalk toward Hope's apartment, her arm linked with Daniel's. How wonderful it was to have him so near, and yet, why was her mind so unsettled?

Maybe it was the silence again. He wasn't to blame for that. As far as they'd walked together, she hadn't ventured a single word. There had been far too much clamor in her mind.

All her life, she'd adhered to the practices of their predominantly Old Order district without wavering. She'd willingly submitted herself to her earthly father, even when others, like the Beachey family, didn't see things nearly as conservatively as she did.

She'd never once thought to question Dat's judgment in the past. But what was this now, weighing so heavily on her? She knew the answer as soon as she asked herself. It was Dat's ardent resistance to the recent softening of the rules about shunning. It was those new allowances that had been brought about through the efforts of Bethany's Uncle Caleb. She'd heard Dat talking about it with Opa at great length, sometimes in distressed whispers.

She had to be honest with herself. It hadn't just been that Dat and Opa had reservations. She'd shared their reluctance, too, especially when the Beacheys had a long lost brother attend a family wedding last month. Of course, this was before she'd known that Aunt Hope existed. She'd had no idea there'd been a shunning in the Bright family, too, much less that Dat and Opa had opposed this very compromise, even with her Aunt Hope in mind. Had she just taken on their convictions without thinking it through for herself?

Daniel pulled her close. She returned the smile he gave her, but as they walked on, her mind continued to turn. She sifted through what she'd overheard about the shunning decision. Why hadn't she paid closer attention?

Bits and pieces drifted back. According to Opa, there had been a spirited debate between the two ministers. That she remembered. Their bishop had struck what Opa viewed as a troubling compromise. Under certain conditions, heads of families could now choose if they'd like to reconnect with formerly shunned relatives. Dat had called it a very slippery slope. At the time, she had firmly agreed.

What were those conditions they'd mentioned? She knit her brow, trying to remember. Oh, yes. It was only permitted if the person was of good reputation. That was one. And there was something about... There. That was the other requirement: the person also had to be involved with an English church. This was especially for Mennonites, like Caleb Beachey's brother had become.

It was the strangest thing. In the past—though Charity had never thought it was her place to voice an opinion about what she'd overheard—she had always stood on her father's side. Inwardly, she'd sincerely shared his concern as the lines had begun to blur between Old and New Amish Orders under the differing convictions of their leadership.

Now, she wasn't entirely sure.

Daniel squeezed her hand. "Are you feeling all right?"

Charity looked up into the night sky. There was no easy way to tell him the truth she'd been holding inside. How could she explain it to him when she still didn't know her own mind? "I'm sorry, Daniel. It's just... It's about Aunt Hope. She's not coming home."

Daniel's brow furrowed. "She told you this?"

"Last night."

He let out a heavy sigh as they turned the final corner to her street. "Perhaps she needs some more encouragement."

Charity knew Daniel well enough to recognize him as a solver. Whatever the problem, he'd want to help her with it. But this problem was beyond his solutions. "Sadly, I don't think so. She's really considered it, and she's made up her mind."

Daniel glanced sidelong at Charity. "I'm surprised you're accepting that so easily."

Something choked in Charity's throat. "Nothing about this is easy for me, Daniel." She turned away, punishing herself. That had come out much more abruptly than she'd intended. "Please forgive me."

"You've done nothing wrong."

Charity shook her head ruefully. There was much more to this than Daniel understood. It gnawed at her stomach, refusing to let go. She prayed for the courage to admit what Gott already knew.

"Wait." Daniel stopped. He turned to face her. "Charity... What is it?"

As much as she fought them, tears blurred her vision. "I've been doubting."

"Doubting what?"

It was so hard to hold his gaze. In all her life, she'd never felt so riddled with uncertainty. How could she admit the truth of what had her so completely undone? On the other hand, how could she have the kind of relationship she wanted with him if she couldn't tell him? She gathered her courage. "I've doubted—well, just about everything. Our whole way of life."

Daniel searched her face. "What are you saying?" He looked so crushed.

"Nothing yet," Charity explained. "I'm still struggling with it. I don't even know what I..."

With that, he took her trembling hands in his. He brushed them with a kiss. "What is there to know? Tomorrow, we take the train home. You'll return to your brothers, your father, and your grandfather. We'll celebrate Christmas with the wonderful secret of how we feel."

Charity swallowed, failing to stem the flow of tears. "But... Daniel, how am I going to say goodbye to her? I'm wondering if I should."

Tenderly, Daniel wiped a tear from her cheek. "We knew this would be hard, Charity."

Charity shook her head. "You don't understand. You have sisters. You grew up with your mother.

She is still the heart of your family. Aunt Hope, she's the closest thing to a mother I have."

"But your Aunt Hope, she is not your mother."

How could she help him to grasp this? She tucked a loose tendril back behind her ear. "I know she's not, Daniel. Even she says how very different they were. But we have a connection now. We're the last two women left in my family. And please understand how painful that bond is to break."

Daniel studied her soberly. Finally, he seemed to recognize the crossroads they had reached. "One connection or the other will be broken. So it will. You realize that."

"That's why this is so hard." Tears coursed down Charity's cheeks. It was not at all like the Amish to give way to such emotion, but try as she might, she could not control what was tearing her apart. "Daniel...help me."

Daniel opened his arms to her. How long he held her, she didn't know. He stroked her back, so patiently, until she quieted. Even then, he waited longer, before he pulled back and looked into her eyes. "Charity, I can love you with everything that is in me. I can pray that it is enough. But that is where I end and you begin. This, you have to decide."

Charity nodded as she wiped her face. Daniel was right. No matter what she chose, her heart would be divided. That much she knew. She had reached the precipice that every person must, that moment of decision. It was a choice that would define just who and what she was to be for the rest of her life.

Bundled head to toe, Hope and Ivan looked out, over the Upper Bay to the Statue of Liberty, illuminated against the starry night sky. What a grand lady she was, shining out there in the harbor. Hope had come to see the landmark on many an occasion, but no visit had ever felt anywhere near as pivotal as this one.

Ivan pointed across the water, toward the statue. "Lady Liberty. All my life, I had heard of her. And there she is." The fog of Ivan's breath dissipated into the air.

As Hope drank in the sight of the statue, her heart warmed despite the chill of the night. "Beautiful, isn't she?"

Ivan nodded fondly. "I said hello to her when I first came here. And soon, I will bid her goodbye." He turned toward Hope, his eyes glistening with affection. "I will still think of her, but not so very often as I will think of you."

Hope smiled thoughtfully. The peace that had eluded her for so many years settled in her spirit. She had made a decision, and though it had been difficult, she knew it was the right one.

"Marry me, Ivan."

Ivan turned to her, stunned.

Hope took his hand in hers, never more sure. "Stay. Build a life with me."

Though, clearly, it was all Ivan could do to process what she was saying, an incredulous joy shimmered in his eyes. His upturned mouth dropped wide open. "You. You are... This is what you want, now?"

Never breaking his gaze, Hope nodded. "This is what I want. Always." Hope drew Ivan toward her and into a soft kiss, communicating all the love she'd found in her heart.

What a joy it was for Hope to share the news of her engagement with Charity and Daniel. Both Ivan and she did their best to exult quietly, so as not to wake Leanne's baby. The child slumbered in a makeshift cradle, a deep dresser drawer set atop her coffee table, lined with soft terry towels.

Leanne threw her arms around Hope and Ivan at the same time. Charity was next. Hope embraced Charity long and hard, knowing how bittersweet this news would be for her. As Hope looked over Charity's shoulder to Daniel, he acknowledged their news kindly, but with a reserve Hope couldn't help detect.

Charity pulled back to arm's length with Hope, overwhelmed. "Oh, Aunt Hope! I am so happy for you."

Ivan appeared between them. "And what about your Uncle to be? Are you happy for him?"

Charity beamed. "I'm going to have an uncle, too?"

"And cousins," Hope added. "Don't forget cousins."

Ivan raised an enthused hand. "Yes! I promise you many cousins."

Noticing her awakened infant, Leanne scooped him up in her arms. "You hear that Jesse-boy? You're not gonna be the only baby around here."

Surprised, Hope turned to Leanne. "You named him?"

Leanne swaddled Jesse. "After my daddy. He and Momma are flyin' in tomorrow, so we can have Christmas together.

Hope's heart leapt. "You called them."

"I did," Leanne smiled.

"Ah, I'm so glad." Hope reached out to give Leanne a big hug. Jesse started to fuss from the commotion.

Leanne bounced him maternally. "It's okay, Sweet Pea. We're just excited."

Charity stepped toward Leanne. "I'll get him."

"Thanks." Leanne put her son into Charity's waiting arms.

Ivan moved toward Charity. "Bring him around this way, Charity. Let me see you with this boy."

Charity soothed little Jesse as she turned him into Ivan's view. "Shhhh... It's all right." The child calmed readily at the sound of Charity's voice.

Ivan seemed impressed. "You are very good with babies." He turned to Leanne. "Look at my niece, how good she is!"

"She is." Leanne opened her arms wide, coaxing Hope's embrace. "Tell you what, Hope. This is gonna be some Christmas."

"Already is," Hope exuded, but as she watched Charity, she noted a hint of sadness in her eyes. Hope exchanged a look with Daniel, concerned. "Daniel..."

Daniel motioned Hope toward the door. "May I speak with you? Downstairs?"

While Charity continued to soothe baby Jesse, Hope quietly followed Daniel out the door.

All the way down the steps into the building's lobby, Hope wondered. What did Daniel have on his mind? In a way, she hated to upset the happiness of the evening, but then again, there was no sense in putting off finding out what was troubling him. "Daniel... Is everything okay?"

Daniel maintained his composure, but the sober look never left his eyes. "You could have waited."

Hope searched his expression. "Waited to...?"

"This is already hard enough for her."

Perplexed, Hope stepped aside from the stairs. "What? To let her see that I'm happy?"

Daniel cleared the way as a matronly woman passed and trudged up the stairs with her wash basket. "You know it is much more than that."

Sensing that her neighbor was listening, Hope deliberately lowered her voice. "Daniel, all right. Okay, I honestly—"

"Do not lie to me." Though Daniel didn't raise his voice, his face was set.

"I wouldn't," Hope promised. "I haven't."

He looked down momentarily before returning to meet her gaze. "Do you want Charity to stay here with you?"

Inside, Hope reeled at the question, knowing no answer would satisfy him. "Of course, I do. She's like my daughter."

"The daughter you abandoned," he specified. "You valued this life with the English more than you valued any of us. Do not forget that."

Nothing about this was going to be easy, Hope realized. It never had been. And despite the fresh assurance she held in her heart about marrying Ivan, she knew it never would be. "Daniel, this isn't fair."

"No, it isn't." He paused, seeming to gather his words. "It is one thing for you to choose this world. It's another for you to play with Charity's emotions."

"Daniel, no. I am not—"

"She is strong, yes. But she is still so sensitive. Do you not see that?"

Hope fought frustration, though it threatened to get the better of her. "Of course, I do."

Daniel shook his head. "In all this time, you have said nothing of the ugliness of the city, nothing of heartache of living with the English. Admit it. You want her to stay. You're afraid to tell her the truth of how desperately alone you've felt, all these years without your family."

How in the world could she respond? His words pierced right through her, all the way to intentions so deep that she hadn't dared admit them to herself. Her cast clunked awkwardly as she leaned against the newel post. "What difference does it make, Daniel? Charity isn't staying. She's going back with you tomorrow."

"You don't know that. You have influenced her."

"And so have you," Hope retorted. "But at least, if she does go home, she'll know I'm settled now. That I'll have family here."

"Yes," Daniel emphasized. "An aunt, an uncle, and soon little cousins out here to miss. And her heart will always be divided. Just exactly the way yours has been."

With everything in her, Hope tried to compose words to defend herself. But not a contrary sentence would form in her mind. He'd been maddeningly spot-on about everything he'd said. He had said it as frankly and respectfully as he could. Worst of all, he was absolutely right. There was no way to fight him any longer.

Suddenly, tears were streaming down her face. Soon, she was sobbing. The pain and grief she'd borne for almost seventeen years rained down. She had known her decision would be painful, but this was sheer agony.

Before Hope knew it, Daniel had wrapped her in his arms. As she felt him softly shaking, she realized he how deeply he empathized. "I'm so sorry. I didn't mean to hurt you."

"I know," Hope whispered. "You love her, too. How could you not?" Hope pulled back. She met Daniel's gaze. "Okay. I'll tell her the truth. I'll step back. This is Charity's choice to make, and I will let her make it."

fifteen

Alone in Hope's room, Charity's gaze lingered on her empty suitcase. It seemed impossible that three weeks had already passed, that the time to return home had come. Then again, it had. Tomorrow, it would be Christmas Eve, the day she'd promised to board the train with Daniel for home.

It wasn't just the disappointment that Aunt Hope had decided not to return with them that kept Charity wandering down trails of thought. That, by itself, was unexpectedly painful. It was the way the experience of living in the city had made her question so many things.

It wasn't the allure of the city that Dat had feared. She could do without electricity. She didn't care about things like driving a car or wearing English clothes. But the more she thought about it, the more she realized there was one thing she would never be able make peace with, ever.

It was saying a final goodbye to Aunt Hope.

A hollow pang rumbled through her. How unsettling it was to differ with Dat for the first time, even in her mind. The solid ground on which she'd always depended quaked beneath her. She tried to imagine explaining it all to Dat, but couldn't. How could she, without breaking his heart?

Then, there was Daniel. She would also need to tell him everything, and pray that he'd understand. Suddenly, her eyes were pooling all over again. There was no question of how she felt about Daniel. She was in love with him. She knew it by the wave of grief that crashed over her the instant she considered what it would be like to lose him.

And lose him, she might.

Daniel's father was a deacon. Along with most others, the Yoders ardently held to the most conservative Old Order persuasions. Daniel had been raised that way, just as she had been. But there was that small, growing minority within their community who were beginning to embrace certain things the Brights and Yoders never had. Bethany's Uncle Caleb and her father, Samuel Beachey, were chief among them.

Charity didn't underestimate how much siding with the Beacheys could affect her relationship with Daniel. She faltered. A single thought drained the strength from her. If they were blessed with children, what would happen when they came of age for Rumspringa? What if a son or daughter of theirs grew up to choose the English world over theirs? Daniel had always been so devout. As head of their household, would he ask her to shun their own child, even a believing one, forever?

Charity brushed her lips lightly, reflecting on Daniel's kiss. This could come to mean their parting. How could she bear to live without him? Yet, for the first time, she began to consider what it would mean to live with him, to be a good wife and a mother to his children. If she became more progressive, he might not want to marry her at all. Neither might anyone else in their predominantly Old Order community.

This was no small thing. It certainly hadn't been for Bethany. As attractive as Bethany was, not a single conservative man had spoken for her. So few had taken the Beachey family's side. It had left Bethany with little hope of finding a like-minded husband, at least inside their district.

It was all so complicated. Sure, Charity wouldn't be entirely alone if she embraced the Beachey's progressive leanings, but then she would quickly find herself in the scant minority along with Bethany. She'd be at unspoken odds with the great majority of their community, including Daniel's family as much as her own.

Charity ran her fingers along her suitcase. How she missed her family. Still, as much as she longed to return to them, how could she go back to life as it had been? If returning meant alienating herself from her family—whether with Dat and Opa or, in time, with Daniel—then perhaps there was no reason to pack her suitcase at all. Then again, how could she stay, if staying meant never seeing anyone at home again? Either way, it would be devastating.

Charity massaged her temples. Somehow, she had to sort this all out in her mind. Time in the city had been nothing like she had imagined. Honestly, she'd expected that the trappings of English life would feel much more like sin than they had.

No wonder Aunt Hope had been so ferhuddled when she first faced this confusing tangle of choices.

Were these modern conveniences, in and of themselves, even sins at all? The more Charity mulled it over, the less important it seemed whether transportation was by carriage or car. It didn't seem to matter whether the lamp that lit a room was oil, kerosene, or fluorescent, or if a stove that cooked their food was wood, propane, or electric. What seemed of greatest consequence was how a thing was used.

Aunt Hope's church was far from Mennonite, let alone Amish. It had been illuminated with countless wired lights, and faces that shone even brighter. Myrna had sung into a microphone accompanied by an electric guitar. The words to the songs had been projected on a screen. Still, she could not deny it. In spite of all that technology, she had experienced Gott's presence there. That she knew. His nearness had been every bit as real to her in that English church as it had been at home, worshipping amongst the Amish.

A question rushed into her heart. It was so simple, yet so resounding that it took her breath away:

If your heavenly Father doesn't shun your Aunt Hope, then how, in good faith, could you?

She sat, motionless, allowing the words to sink down to her innermost being. Would she follow her traditions, or would she follow Gott? There would be no turning back once she answered that question. The magnitude of it left her trembling. Reverently, Charity bowed her head. Silently, she vowed:

I will follow Your example, whatever that means.

Peace flooded her. It encircled her, like a blanketing embrace. No matter what happened, she would not be alone.

It wasn't long before Charity heard the familiar creak of Aunt Hope's bedroom door and the padding of her footsteps as she entered. Her reverie broken, she looked up from the still empty suitcase. "Did Ivan leave so soon?"

Hope approached. "He did. He said he wanted us to have this last night together."

Charity smiled affectionately. "He's a good man, my uncle to be."

"Yes," Hope agreed. "He is."

Wistfully, Charity rose. "I need to pack, but I guess I'm having a bit of trouble getting started." Charity picked up the borrowed uniform with its lengthened skirt. "I suppose I should hem this back up for you tonight."

Aunt Hope selected a hanger from her closet. "No, no." With a fond smile, she draped the garment across it. "Actually, I think I'd like to wear it this way. To remember you."

As Aunt Hope hung the uniform on her closet bar, Charity saw her hesitate. Her gaze seemed fixed on a shoebox on the shelf in front of her. After a moment, she reached up and pulled the shoebox down. She carried it into the bathroom and wiped the gathered dust off the top.

Aunt Hope returned with the shoebox, a contemplative expression on her face. She sat on the bed. "That Christmas card of mine you brought back this year... I guess you never read it."

Charity shook her head. "It was addressed to Dat, so no. I never opened it."

"You should," Aunt Hope suggested. She cradled the box in her hands. "You should read that one, and there are more here, too. One for every Christmas I've been gone."

As Aunt Hope lifted the top off the box, she revealed a stack of cards. They were all stamped *Return to Sender*. "I don't mean to mislead you. It has been so hard here. Desperately." Aunt Hope's eyes dampened. "Hard in ways I guess I could only express to my brother in these cards. Maybe because I knew he'd never read them. He'd never know how spectacularly broken I've been." Slowly, Aunt Hope extended the box of returned cards toward Charity.

Respectfully, Charity resisted. "I shouldn't."

Again, Aunt Hope handed over the box. "No, Sweetheart. Trust me. You should."

Charity searched Aunt Hope's eyes. It was as if she could see right through them, all the way to the utter loneliness of her soul. In a way, like the words of that carol they had sung about Bethlehem, the hopes and fears of all the years did seem to be met in these Christmas cards. They must be too personal, too intimate, and yet Aunt Hope appeared somehow relieved when Charity reached out to accept the box.

Charity waited quietly. It seemed best to let Aunt Hope leave the room. When the door closed, she sat back down on the bed.

Where to begin?

Sorting through the stack of cards, Charity's eyes settled on the very earliest of the postmarks.

That was where she'd start. She would experience the passing of the years in the same order that her Aunt Hope had lived them, one lonesome Christmas after another.

By the time Charity returned to the living room, a full hour had passed. Aunt Hope was helping Daniel make up the couch for his final night there.

Leanne padded across the apartment in fuzzy socked feet, towards her room. She cradled baby Jesse in her arms. "Night-night everybody. Come on, Smokey." The cat sauntered behind her, surprisingly compliant.

Hope shot a smile in Leanne's direction. "Sleep well." She turned to Daniel. "Just one more night on the sofa. I know it'll feel good to get back home to a real bed."

What had privately passed between Aunt Hope and Daniel, Charity didn't know for sure, but from the way Daniel thanked Aunt Hope as she headed off to bed, it seemed they must have resolved it. Perhaps it had been about the cards. Or it could have been something more. Maybe both of them knew how torn she had been between them, and the places they called home.

Finally alone, Charity and Daniel stood silently for a moment. As much thought as Charity had put into what she wanted to say, it was still hard to know exactly where to begin.

Daniel set a pillow in place on the sofa, and then straightened up to face her. "Before you say anything, please know two things: whatever you do tomorrow is your choice, Charity. And whether you stay or return with me, whatever you decide, know that I will always love you."

Charity felt her eyes fill as she met his searching gaze.

"Talk to me, Charity. Please. I want to know everything you've been thinking and feeling."

Something in those words meant the world to Charity. Daniel was a man of great conviction, yes. But he was also a man who would sincerely listen to her. She wouldn't have to hide her emotions, as her people usually did. He wasn't just saying that she would have a voice in their relationship. He was demonstrating that she would. It made it somehow easier to pour it all out, to unburden herself of every secret thought that had been stirring in her mind.

How long it was that Daniel stood listening, Charity couldn't say. All she knew was that he never once interrupted her, nor made any attempt to invalidate what she had been thinking. On a few points, it actually seemed that he might be inclined to agree with her, even when it came to learning of her less than conservative Amish leanings.

Her cheeks were streaked by the time she reached her conclusion. "It's not about choosing whether or not to live in the city. It's not about technology. She's family, Daniel. I love her. I want to write to her, to call her. I want us to be able to visit. And if that somehow distances me from my family back home, then I don't know. Maybe I'll see if I can move in with Bethany's family, since I think they would allow it."

Daniel's brow rose. "You'd leave your father's house?"

"If I have to," Charity nodded. "I understand if this is too much for you, Daniel. I can't tell you how it breaks my heart to say it. But if this is something that you can't accept along with who I'm realizing that I've become...then as much as I love you, I can't keep seeing you. And I cannot be your wife."

Daniel glanced down momentarily, seeming to gather his words. Finally, he looked up. "You're not the only one who has been doing some serious soul searching, Charity." Daniel brushed a hand over his face. A moment passed before he could bring himself to speak. When he did, his voice caught in his throat. "I cannot lose you needlessly, Charity. Not like your father lost your mother."

Charity stood, stunned. Was he saying what she thought he was? "You would take me to an English hospital."

"I would." Daniel paused. "It's about more than that, though. It was just...seeing you deliver Leanne's baby. So calm, so assured. It made me think what a good midwife you could be, if only you could get some training."

Charity brightened. "Really? Oh, Daniel. I never dreamed... I can't tell you how happy that would make me." She wrapped her arms around him.

Holding her close, Daniel whispered. "What we do under our fathers' rooftops is one thing, Charity. It would be wrong to disrespect them while we're there. But all during this coming year, I'll be building a new house, with a new roof to cover us. What we decide to do there, we can decide for ourselves. Together."

Charity pulled back. She searched Daniel's eyes longingly. "Are you sure?"

"I know it seems like a long time till the next harvest, but out of respect for our fathers, I'm asking if you can wait."

His eyes looked so earnest, so patient, so true. Everything in her conflicted heart rested at the sight of him. "I know this has been hard for you, too— me being so torn—and you not knowing what I would do." Charity stroked his face tenderly. She felt the light stubble along the squareness of his jaw. "I so dearly respect it that you fought for me and still, you gave me the room I needed to choose."

Daniel smiled at her lovingly, his eyes still glistening.

Charity took his hands in hers. "I choose you, Daniel Yoder. Ivan is her home, now, and you are mine. Above all others, I choose you."

Christmas Eve found holiday travelers bustling through Penn Station, laden with baggage. Many toted festively wrapped gifts. The station was even more crowded than when they had come.

Hope and Ivan led Charity and Daniel through the throng, toward their train's scheduled platform. Leanne and baby Jesse weren't far behind.

Hope pointed out an electronic sign, posting their destination. "Guess that's you, huh?

Charity stopped. She looked back longingly. "I'm afraid so."

Aunt Hope handed a sack to Charity. "Rhubarb. So you can make a pie for my brother, Nathan. Our secret that it's from me."

"Yes, so it is. Our secret." Charity accepted the fruit appreciatively. "He'll love it, I know."

Ivan extended a parcel to Daniel. "Would you carry this for her?"

"It's your Christmas present, Charity." Hope's eyes shone. "But open it, as soon as you're on the train."

For a moment, Charity fretted. "But I have nothing for you."

"You have already given me so much, Charity, just by coming here. I can't ever thank you enough for that. Just take this. I want you to have it."

"All right, then. I'm sure that, whatever it is, I'll treasure it." As Daniel tucked the parcel under his arm, Charity smiled warmly at Ivan. "Goodbye, Uncle. Take good care of her."

Ivan tipped his head. "I promise."

Charity took Aunt Hope's hand. "Daniel and I have talked about it and—once we're married, under our own roof—I hope that you'll write to me."

Aunt Hope's eyes widened. She checked with Daniel to make sure. He nodded his approval. "You'll read my letters?"

Charity beamed. "Quietly, for Dat's sake. And I will open and answer every one of them."

Aunt Hope put a cast-laden hand to her heart. "Oh, Charity. I know how much this means."

"That's not all, Aunt Hope," Charity continued. Next Christmas, we hope you and Ivan will come and celebrate at our table. Perhaps by then we can persuade Dat and Opa to join us."

Aunt Hope threw her arms around Charity.

Charity relished the embrace. "What is done in faith is not sin, Aunt Hope. And loving you could never be a sin to me."

As they finally parted, Aunt Hope tenderly kissed Charity's cheek. A rosy smudge of her lipstick remained. Aunt Hope used her good thumb to rub it away as best she could.

Leanne let out a hoot. "Whoops, everybody. Think I see an Amish girl with lipstick on."

Charity traded grins with Leanne, then drew the ribbon of Aunt Hope's kapp across her neck affectionately. "Right here. That's how close we'll be yet."

"Right here."

Charity returned a kiss to Aunt Hope's cheek. "Till next Christmas."

"Yes," Aunt Hope smiled. "Next Christmas."

Charity tore herself away. She hurried with Daniel toward the train. They slipped through the automatic doors, just before they slid to a close.

As they walked down the aisle, Charity drank in a final look through the window at those they were leaving there. Ivan put an arm around Aunt Hope as she tearfully waved goodbye. Leanne raised Jesse's tiny hand to wave, too.

Charity and Daniel took their seats just as the train began to roll away. Unable to stave off her curiosity any longer, Charity peeked into the parcel that Daniel had set down at their feet. There was the Bright family tree quilt that Aunt Hope had made. A handwritten note was pinned to the top of it. It read:

Add to this, Charity, as our family tree grows.
I love you forever.

Your devoted Aunt Hope

Overwhelmed, Charity turned to look back out their window.

Aunt Hope followed them down the platform, still waving. Her eyes shimmering with gratitude, Charity pressed her hand to the glass until they were long out of sight. With her other hand, she held Daniel's. They would not be able to hold hands like this much longer, at least not in public. So, she kept her hand in his, all the way out of the city, across the state line, and into the rolling hills of Pennsylvania.

Never could Charity remember a time that her heart was so full. It had not been torn in two, as she had feared. Instead, it was as if it had been enlarged somehow, reaching beyond the borders they crossed in either direction.

What a wonderful adventure this trip had been, every last moment of it. As the train glided along, she reflected on all the pictures that she had taken in her mind. They were memories that would last her until the next Christmas, when they would all be together as a family once again.

Charity sighed happily. Daniel dozed at her side, his fingers still laced with hers. Never once had he complained, but apparently, so many nights on Aunt

Hope's sofa had left him shy on sleep. He had given so freely of himself the whole three weeks, even toward Leanne.

By noon, Leanne's parents would have arrived at the Café Troubadour. They'd be reunited with their long-lost daughter. They'd meet their baby grandson, Jesse, for the very first time. Just to think of their reunion brought a smile to her face.

Hope and Myrna would be caroling to the café's lunch crowd, blending in perfect harmony. Goldie would be ordering a tuna melt, insisting that his crinkle-cut fries should be very well done. Shep's fingers would be dancing across the ivories as his guide dog lounged under his bench. Ivan would be washing dishes till they sparkled, making Frank glad that he had the good sense to hire him. Maybe Frank would even let him cook in time.

How beautifully everything had worked out for Aunt Hope and Ivan. Soon, they would be married. Their lives would find a new rhythm in the city, and she would always have been a part of that. What a privilege it seemed.

As hard as it had been to leave, a lightness filled her spirit about going back. The farther they traveled, the more she longed for the familiar fields of home. Dat, Opa, Aaron, and Isaac would be waiting for them at the train station in town. Bethany would surely be there, too. She'd be there with those shining eyes of hers, bobbing on her toes, waiting to hear every last detail about absolutely everything that had happened. How she'd missed all of them, and how right it felt to be returning with Daniel to the life she loved so well.

Before bedtime, she'd start preparing Christmas dinner. Opa would have a turkey ready to dress and roast overnight. In the morning, there would be fresh curly kale from the garden, and yams to make with that brown sugar-cinnamon with oats topping her brothers always craved. She would think of Aunt Hope as she cut up the rhubarb to make Dat's very favorite pie.

Daniel stirred beside her with the jostling of the train. He brushed her arm fondly before his eyes fluttered back to a close. What a good man he was, and how assured she felt of his love. It would be her joy to marry him, to make a home and life together, to add to their family tree.

Lightly, Charity ran her fingers along the ribbons of Aunt Hope's kapp, knowing that, in their spirits, they were still together. And they would be, she reminded herself, until next Christmas found them feasting at their table.

As Charity drank in the passing landscape, a soft snow began to fall. Somehow she knew that, far across the miles, Aunt Hope would be singing the very same song that rose in her own brimming heart.

Daniel slept at her side, in what could only be described as heavenly peace. This Christmas night would, indeed, be both silent and holy. All was so calm, so full of wonder and promise, and at the same time, so radiantly bright.

About the Author

SUSAN ROHRER is an honor graduate of James Madison University where she studied Art and Communications, and thereafter married in her native state of Virginia.

A professional writer, producer, and director specializing in life-affirming entertainment, Rohrer's credits in one or more of these capacities include: a screen adaptation of *God's Trombones;* 100 episodes of drama series *Another Life;* Humanitas Prize finalist & Emmy winner *Never Say Goodbye;* Emmy nominees *Terrible Things My Mother Told Me* and *The Emancipation of Lizzie Stern;* anthology *No Earthly Reason;* NAACP Image Award nominee *Mother's Day;* AWRT Public Service Award winner (for addressing the problem of teen sexual harassment) *Sexual Considerations;* comedy series *Sweet Valley High;* telefilms *Book of Days,* and *Another Pretty Face;* Emmy nominee & Humanitas Prize finalist *If I Die Before I Wake;* as well as Film Advisory Board & Christopher Award winner *About Sarah.*

Among the other books she has authored, Rohrer's fictional titles, *Merry's Christmas, Virtually Mine,* and *What Laurel Sees* are also part of the REDEEMING ROMANCE Series of inspirational love stories adapted from Rohrer's original screenplays.

Note: *Out of respect for Amish sensibilities, the author has chosen not to include a personal photograph in this book*

OTHER REDEEMING ROMANCES BY SUSAN ROHRER

Merry's Christmas: a love story

Desperate to make ends meet, winsome diner waitress Merry Hopper takes a temporary job as a Christmas Coordinator to a handsome banker, promising to bring Christmas back for his three kids. As the "haves" collide with the "have nots" of this world, Merry finds herself head over heels for the family she's never had—most of all her new banker boss—not realizing that he's well on the way toward a Yuletide engagement with his employer's beautiful daughter.

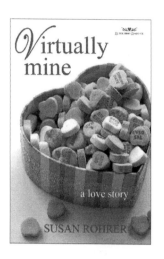

Virtually Mine: a love story

Devastated to think that she's lost her steady beau to another ingénue, aspiring actress Kate Valentine consoles herself by renting an Imaginary Boyfriend from burgeoning romance broker *Virtually Mine*. Kate's Imaginary Boyfriend sends her flowers. He calls. He texts sweet nothings, plucking at her heartstrings. As the lines between make-believe and reality blur, Kate finds herself longing for true love, never knowing that it could be much closer than she thinks.

What Laurel Sees: a love story

A Redeeming Romance Mystery

When Laurel Fischer has a disturbing vision that precedes her ex-husband's slaying, Laurel seems a likely suspect. The harder Laurel fights to get custody of her daughter back, the more that spells motive to authorities.

A reluctant rag sheet reporter, Joe Hardisty, is pegged to cover the story, focusing on Laurel's visionary gift. As skeptical about relationships as he is about matters of faith, Joe's walls are high, but the enigmatic Laurel unearths his most closely guarded secrets. A forbidden romance blossoms as this mystery unfolds and detectives close in on a killer.

NONFICTION BY SUSAN ROHRER

THE HOLY SPIRIT: Spiritual Gifts
Amazing Power for Everyday People

IS GOD SAYING
HE'S THE ONE?
*Hearing From Heaven About
That Man in Your Life*

SECRETS OF THE DRY BONES
Ezekiel 37:1–14
The Mystery of a Prophet's Vision

A Final Note
Before We Say Goodbye

Dear Reader,

Thanks so much for the time we've spent together as you've read this book. I hope you enjoyed reading it as much as I did writing it.

Would you consider posting a quick review? It's easy. Just go to the review section of this book's page on Amazon. You'll get to share your reading experience with family, friends, as well as other readers across the world, and I'll truly appreciate your feedback.

Gratefully,
Susan Rohrer

15515969R00158

Made in the USA
Middletown, DE
09 November 2014